I0633025

Mine To Avenge
A Steve Dane Thriller

Brian Drake

WOLFPACK
PUBLISHING
— EST 2013 —

Text copyright © 2021 (As Revised) Brian Drake

Published by Wolfpack Publishing
5130 S. Fort Apache Road, 215-380
Las Vegas, NV 89148

Paperback IBSN 978-1-64734-741-3
eBook ISBN 978-1-64734-740-6

Mine To Avenge

This one is for Leslie Charteris,
because the world still needs a saint,
and still offers romance and adventure
for those who know where to look.

PART ONE

PART ONE

Chapter One

The nightmare again.

Nina Talikova stood in a dark room with only a spot of light ahead of her, partially illuminating a man standing in front of a desk. She did not approach. Her heartrate increased as she looked for an exit but found none. The darkness was on either side and behind her. The only light was in front of her. The man leaned his face into the light.

"Nina."

She frowned at the man as his features began to take shape.

"Nina."

"No," she said. "Never."

The man straightened, the light leaving his face, but still highlighting a portion of his dark suit.

The man said nothing more.

Nina looked left, right, furiously, for an escape, and her legs felt like lead when she tried to move.

"Soon," the man said.

Nina jerked awake in bed, the pillow and covers damp with sweat as she pushed the blankets away and sat up. She looked at Steve Dane, lying beside her on his stomach. He breathed steadily, quietly, while Nina's heart raced.

The hotel room in Bonn, Germany, was dark but little slivers of light from outside streetlamps pierced the curtains. She could move freely now and proved it by leaving the bed and wandering into the bathroom for a gulp of water from a plastic cup. She ran a washcloth under cold water and wiped her face and neck, and consciously tried not to make eye contact with herself in the mirror. To do so might mean admitting she knew the identity of the man in her dream. Nina had made it her goal to never see the man again, but there would be no avoiding a confrontation.

A final one, at that.

Soon.

Just like he said.

Nina flicked off the bathroom light and returned to bed.

The black Chevrolet sedan jumped the curb, plowed over the mailbox, and gouged a deep rut in the grass, but Sam Roca never took his foot from the accelerator. He finally slammed the brakes only steps from the front door of the dark house.

He shut off the car and started coughing, the rough spasm sending barbs of pain throughout his body, and he paused just a moment to look at the spatter of blood he'd sprayed on the steering wheel. A look down at the wound in his side showed no let-up in the bleeding. Time was running out if he didn't act fast.

Roca shoved open the door, grabbing his half-empty pistol from the passenger seat. He started for the front door, fell on the hard concrete of the walkway, and struggled to hands and knees. More coughing, more pain, more blood clogging from his throat. He spit to clear his mouth but the taste remained. Less time than he thought. Roca gained his feet and staggered for the door, leaving a red trail from the car to the front steps.

The key didn't slip from his bloody left hand and he pushed the door open, closed it behind him, and sank against the solid oak. He slid down to land on his rear end and tried to breathe deep but even that hurt, and the air didn't seem to get to his lungs anyway. He rolled to his left, crawled across the marble entryway to the carpet of the front sitting room and from there maneuvered around furniture to the fireplace. He pulled open the gate and dug into his jacket pockets.

He produced folded sheets of paper and a small notebook, all of which went into the fireplace. He held back one sheet and, with a Zippo, finally lit the paper on fire, placing it with the rest. He watched while the flame caught. Soon the items were ablaze, and nothing would bring them back to life. His next goal wouldn't be so easy. He lay on his side gasping for breath.

He wanted a moment, just a moment, to stop and rest, but the killers weren't far behind. He used a table for leverage and stood up, swaying a little. Gripping his pistol tightly, he moved across the front room, down a hallway, into a den. There he opened a wall safe, removed a flat leather case, and took it over to a desk. He placed the case on the desktop sat down hard, removing a pair of scissors from a drawer along with three envelopes and a package of stamps. He played through the scenario in his head. He could burn the notebook and the other clues, but he couldn't burn the map inside the leather case.

He opened the case and slipped out the map. It was crudely drawn but accurate enough to kill over.

He picked up the scissors and cut the map into four pieces. Two pieces went into one envelope, single pieces in the other two.

Dick "Skinner" McNab said, "Slow down."

The driver pressed on the brakes. "There he is," the driver, a New Jersey gunman named Frost, said.

"Might as well have put up a neon sign," Skinner said.

Frost drove past the house, parking the car further up the road. He and Skinner climbed out, their long coats covering the silenced Uzi submachine guns slung under their arms. It was the perfect place for a showdown, high in the hills outside town, plenty of overgrowth from the surrounding forest to hide in. They walked back to Roca's house. The front yard itself had not been taken care of and some of the forest had crossed over. Skinner examined Roca's Chevy, saw the blood in the driver's seat, and with his eyes followed the trail to the front steps.

Frost said, "I'm surprised he didn't die."

"Better this way," Skinner said.

Another engine broke the night's silence, the sound growing as the vehicle neared. Skinner and Frost ran for cover and dropped flat. The car pulled into the driveway. The driver hopped out, took only a second to look at the Chevy, drew a gun and ran into the house.

"Now Wexler's here too," Skinner said.

"Goodie," said Frost.

Chapter Two

Tom Wexler slammed the front door and shouted, "Sam!"

Nothing.

"Sam!"

He saw the blood trail leading to the fireplace. Whatever he had torched still smoldered, wisps of smoke drifting across the room.

"Sam!"

Through the kitchen, living room, down the hall to the den.

He stopped in the doorway. Sam Roca, still in the chair, aimed his gun directly at Wexler's middle.

Wexler put up his hands. "Whoa!"

"I don't trust anybody right now," Roca said. "Put that gun down."

"Sam, come on, we don't have time for this! They ambushed me at the rendezvous!"

"Put your gun down, Tom."

"You need help."

"I'm not telling you again, Tom."

"Sam, we don't have time for this. They're coming."

"Maybe they're here right now. You don't look shot to me."

"You should see the other guy," Wexler said.

Roca coughed, doubling over. Wexler stepped forward. Roca sprang up with his gun, but his right hand was shaking.

"I'm not the enemy, Sam. We gotta get out of here. If I wanted you dead, I wouldn't have bothered to talk."

Roca finally nodded. "I burned the notebook and the other papers."

"Okay."

"We gotta get the map out of here."

Wexler saw the open safe. "Where is it?"

"My jacket. Here." He took out two of the envelopes and passed them to Wexler. "We mail the pieces to the others. They'll take over."

"You'll be there with them. We both will. Come on."

The front door crashed open.

Frost fired into the front door, shattering the locks. His silenced Uzi made only clicking noises as the firing mechanism cycled. Skinner kicked in the door and entered, Frost following.

Frost cut left through the living room while Skinner turned right. Wexler fired from the den's doorway, driving Skinner back. Skinner dropped flat, firing a burst, and crawled left. He took cover near the couch. He smelled smoke, looked at the fireplace. Whatever had burned wasn't the size of the map. He called out to Frost, "Down the side hall!"

He leaned out, firing a burst, stitching the far wall to the right of the front door. It was too dark to see any movement in that area. Pistol shots crashed from elsewhere. Skinner presumed Frost returned fire but couldn't hear over the loud cracks of the unsilenced handgun. More pistol shots and a scream. Exit Frost.

Skinner rose, keeping low, and moved from the view of the entryway to a second doorway off the front room. Then Wexler stepped through with Frost's Uzi. Skinner dropped and rolled as Wexler let a burst go, the shots punching through walls and furniture, nicking Skinner's coat. Skinner returned fire, peppering the doorway, but Wexler had gone.

Skinner jumped up and ran through the doorway into the kitchen. He saw the side hallway. He fired into the darkness there. No return fire. He stayed put and tried to listen for where Wexler had moved to. No sign of Roca. Was he already dead?

Tom Wexler stayed on the floor in the den, covering the hall with the stolen Uzi.

Roca, on the floor near the chair behind Wexler, breathed heavily. "Tom, I'm not gonna make it."

"We both will."

"Tom."

Wexler pried his eyes away and saw Roca crawling toward him, holding the remaining envelope. "Get to a mailbox. Give me that weapon and I'll cover you."

"Sam—"

A burst from Skinner chopped the doorway, shreds of wood flying into the room.

"He's getting closer, Tom."

Tom grabbed the envelopes and handed Roca the Uzi.

"Grenades in the safe," Roca said.

"Now you tell me."

Wexler jumped up, grabbed the two grenades from the back of the safe. Roca edged to the doorway and fired into the kitchen, two blind bursts that didn't connect with flesh. Wexler lobbed one of the grenades around the corner. The explosion shook the house. Wexler leapt out of the room without a goodbye glance, made the front door, and slipped out.

Roca kept the Uzi up, waiting.

Time ticked by.

Footsteps along the hall.

"Sam."

"Skinner."

"Nice try with the pineapple," Skinner said. He stepped into view. Roca tried to hold the Uzi up, but his strength failed. The weapon dropped from his hands.

Roca said, "You'll never catch him."

Skinner smiled. "Don't be so sure."

"Get it over with."

"Nash sends his regards."

Roca's eyes widened, his mouth dropping open. Skinner McNab fired through Roca's open mouth and left the mess behind.

Tom Wexler steered carefully down the curving two-lane road, headlights bright, cursing the eternity it was taking to get to the main road. But taking the road at speed would be just as dangerous as the battle at the house. If he had any chance at all of getting the envelopes in the mail, he had to survive the drive.

His pistol and the last grenade sat on the passenger seat. He kept glancing in the rearview mirror. Skinner wouldn't rest until he had the map. The fight wasn't over.

He worked the wheel left and right as the curves dictated, straying into the opposite lane often, but quickly correcting. He also didn't need a head-on collision. When he saw the headlights behind him, he stepped a little harder on the gas.

Shots peppered the back of the car, smacking through the back glass. Wexler clenched his jaw and leaned forward. More shots followed but they left sparks on the asphalt, Skinner trying for the tires. Wexler straightened the wheel as the road straightened, speeding up, Skinner's car gaining. Wexler grabbed the last grenade and took his other hand off the wheel long enough to pull the pin. He slowed for a turn, wrenched the wheel right. As Skinner completed the turn, Wexler dropped the pineapple out the window and pressed the accelerator.

The shock of the blast almost pushed the car off the road, but Wexler steered into the opposite lane to avoid going over the side. Finally, he reached the man road, turned right toward town, and sped up over 50. It was late enough that there were no other cars on the road, in front or behind him. Some of the hillside was on fire, but he had no idea if Skinner survived the blast. He also wasn't going back to check.

Wexler kept driving for another forty-five minutes. He stopped long enough to drop the envelopes in different mailboxes, driving several blocks in between stops. He pulled into a deserted business park and dialed a number on his cell.

A woman answered.

Chapter Three

"Holly," Wexler said, "they found us. I don't know how but they found us. They killed Sam but I got away. Get to the airport with the tickets. I'll meet you there. Don't argue with me, honey. Just leave. Now."

He broke the connection before Holly could say anything more and dialed a second number.

Voicemail. Wexler cursed but there was no other way. He knew Steve would get the message. "Steve, it's Tom. SOS, buddy. I need your help."

Steve Dane entered the United States via San Francisco International Airport with a passport showing his real name. But as he stepped off the plane from Germany and cleared customs, he wondered if that had been the wisest move. Tom had sent an SOS, and that meant trouble, the kind Dane responded to, but his real name made waves. With the kind of trouble Tom might be in, making waves might do more harm than good.

He'd find out soon enough.

He scanned faces in the crowd as he walked into the

busy baggage collection terminal. A man in a long, rumpled overcoat caught his eye. He went over to the man.

"You haven't changed one bit," Dane told the man.

Tom Wexler smiled back. "Neither have you. You're wearing more money than I've seen all year."

Wexler, as always, looked like a half-made bed with the rumpled overcoat and uneven beard. His thick brown hair sat on his head like a wet mop. Dane stood before him with his hair trimmed close to his skull, sporting a long-sleeved blue silk Vermucci shirt with pearl buttons down the front, still perfectly pressed after the long flight, and black Mick Marten slacks, the creases still in place, with a leather belt. The belt, a little thicker than those commonly worn, contained the cash Dane always carried as a back-up to what he brought in his wallet. The belt contained ten-thousand dollars.

"Get your bags," Wexler said. "We have a ton to talk about."

Presently Dane and Wexler approached a gray BMW M3 convertible with the top down. A jet roared overhead.

"When does Nina get here?" Wexler said.

"Hopefully soon. I left her in Germany to finish a job."

"You left her there?"

"Todd McConn is with her. It's a child recovery gig. The baddies snatched the son of a football consultant."

"How is Todd these days?"

"Still dresses like a cowboy."

"That's our Todd."

Wexler opened the trunk of the BMW and Dane loaded his suitcases inside.

"Nice wheels."

"Bought it used as soon as I got here," Wexler said. "It's my replacement for the one that got shot up the other night."

"Standard transmission?"

"What else is there?"

Dane dropped into the leather passenger seat. Scratches and scuffs dotted the dash. Wexler fired up the motor and they hit the freeway with the V8 rumbling.

Wexler settled on a cruising speed of 75. The rake of the windshield eliminated most of the wind noise and when he spoke Dane had no trouble hearing.

"We're on a treasure hunt, Steve. Biggest ever."

"What is it?"

"Antiques looted from Iraq during and after the war. That place is a free-for-all for smugglers. They get their hands on this stuff and stash it all over the world to sell later. I plugged in with a group trying to recover the artifacts and get them back where they belong."

"Who?"

"A fellow named Sam Roca was in charge. Old soldier and bounty hunter."

"Never heard of him."

"He's dead."

Wexler gave Dane a rundown of what happened at Roca's house, the mailed map pieces, and brief details of the three men to whom those envelopes were addressed.

"The first connection is here in SF," Wexler said. "Name's Meyer. One of Roca's financiers. The other two are in Las Vegas and a town in Arizona."

"So we need to find the associates, put the map back together, and get the loot back where it belongs?"

"And not get killed in the process."

"Know the enemy?"

"I didn't get far enough to know the ones in charge, but I know their thugs. You do, too."

Dane frowned.

"Joe Thorne."

"He's still alive?"

"Still alive, still short, still a pain in the neck, and still running around with Skinner McNab. McNab killed Roca. I think I got him with a grenade, but I'm not sure."

"You can never be sure with that animal."

They were familiar names that Dane had not heard in a long time. Dane had once operated a mercenary outfit called the 30-30 Battalion. Wexler had been a member, so had Thorne and McNab. But Joe Thorne and Skinner McNab were the problem children. Dane had eventually kicked them out.

"Tell me more," Dane said.

"That's it."

"There has to be more, Tom. Thorne and Skinner don't play for peanuts. I'm sure there's money in selling stolen antiques, but it will not be enough for those two. Where's the money they get from the sale going?"

Wexler let out a sigh.

"Where?"

"You're gonna hit the roof if I tell you, Steve."

"I'm waiting."

"Thorne and Skinner are part of a human trafficking syndicate."

"I knew it was something," Dane said.

"Problem is, the US government has been seriously cracking down globally on human trafficking operations, to the point where many of them are hurting or out of business."

"Thorne's especially?"

"Dearly so," Wexler said. "They're desperate for the antiques because the money from the sale means they can prop up their operations for another few months."

"And if not?"

"Who knows? Those who can will pack up and find other things to do, but what about the victims? They'll be abandoned, left to die, horrible stuff like that."

"I know it all too well," Dane said.

"So, yeah, Roca's group was engaged primarily with recovering the antiques, but choking Thorne's syndicate to death was part of our plan too."

Now it was Steve Dane's turn to let out a breath. He was glad Nina wasn't present to hear Wexler's story. The topic was a sensitive one for her, and he wanted to deliver the details personally.

"I'm sorry Roca's gone," Dane said, "but we'll pick up where he left off. Where did his map come from?"

"We found the antiques in Iraq but Thorne and his crew were on our tail. When we found out why they needed them so badly, we shipped them as far away as we could, here to the US. We wanted to keep them on the run and maybe take them out of play while their own network starved. Sam made the map after burying the antiques in Montana."

"So you already know where the antiques are?"

"I wasn't there to help bury them, no."

"But Thorne followed you to the US regardless."

"Yup." Wexler's hands tightened on the wheel. "Look, Steve, I didn't mean to involve you in the grand scheme. I wouldn't presume—"

"Hey," Dane said. "You know me."

Wexler nodded. "That I do. Seriously, Thorne's boss is on the ropes. If Thorne fails, the misfortune would shut the man down for good."

"Who's the boss?"

"That's still a mystery."

"Uh-huh."

Wexler said, "As soon as we get you to your hotel, I'm taking you to meet Holly, and then we get started."

"Who's Holly?"

"My lady." Wexler cracked a smile.

Chapter Four

Wexler swung off the freeway and drove along The Embarcadero. The smelly breeze, a mixture of sweet-salt spray from the bay and putrid sewer fumes from the street, smacked Dane in the face.

"I hate this town," he said.

"You get used to it, actually."

The massive gray Bay Bridge, connecting one side of the bay to the other, stretched before them. Boats sailed under the bridge. Dane and Wexler joined Embarcadero traffic and watched joggers along either side of the road as the traffic inched along.

"Is Joe in town yet?" Dane said.

"He should be. They've known almost every move we've made, Steve."

"You have a leak somewhere."

"And it ain't the plumbing."

Wexler turned off The Embarcadero, drove one block, and stopped under the canopied entrance to a Hyatt hotel. Dane hopped out and retrieved his bags. Wexler handed the keys to a valet and followed Dane inside. The lobby was huge, mostly open floor with a bar and sitting area sectioned off. The high ceiling stretched forever.

The skinny brunette behind the check-in counter wore a shell of make-up that did not crack under the pressure of her smile. Dane checked-in using a credit card; the girl scanned her computer screen and said: "Welcome back, Mr. Dane."

"It's been a while."

Dane signed the check-in form. The girl smiled and handed him a pair of key cards and Dane and Wexler stepped into an elevator nestled in a glass tube. The elevator car shot upward so quickly, the lobby floor falling away equally as fast, that Dane grabbed the support bar. Wexler stood still.

Dane did not examine the two-room suite. He instead entered the bedroom and placed his suitcases on the bed. He removed the X-ray proof bottom of one case. Dane withdrew a leather shoulder harness. A stainless-steel semi-automatic pistol also waited in the compartment, a .45-caliber Detonics Scoremaster.

Dane slipped his arms through the harness and secured the straps to his belt, inserted the pistol into the spring clip holster. The gun hung suspended under his left armpit. His jacket completely covered the rig.

"I can't believe you still use those old guns. Would it kill you to get a Glock?" Wexler said.

Dane frowned at his friend. "Would it kill you to get a haircut?"

Wexler laughed. "Come on, we're gonna be late."

"Looks like we picked up a tail," Wexler said.

They'd been driving for ten minutes, deeper into the city, going up and down hills and getting away from the Bay stink.

"How many?"

"One car," Wexler said.

Dane took out his gun and snapped back the slide. Upping the safety switch, he tucked the gun under his leg.

"This ain't the place for a battle," Wexler said. Traffic was moderate and the humanity on the sidewalk and the buildings on either side of the street lowered their escape and evasion options. It also limited the opposition's choices, but that didn't mean they would hold their fire.

"Turn left up here," Dane said. "Then the next left."

"Back to The Embarcadero?"

"China Basin will give us room to fight."

"I can lose them."

"Not in this traffic."

Wexler swung left, sped down the next street, and screeched the tires in low gear as he made the second left. The shimmering bay water lay ahead, but it was downhill all the way. Wexler shifted to neutral and used the brakes to control his speed, weaving around other cars, zipping briefly into opposing lanes. The road flattened out at each intersection before the downward slope continued. Dane watched the opposition keep up but not get closer.

"Easy, Tommy," he said. "SF's finest are always around the corner."

"Maybe they'll catch the ungodly first," Wexler said.

The road flattened out as they neared The Embarcadero; Wexler turned right, throwing the M3 into third, and raced along the two-lane road. The Bay Bridge loomed ahead, growing larger as they approached. The span momentarily blocked both sun and sky as they passed beneath.

"Straight ahead," Dane said. He looked back. "Down!"

Automatic weapons crackled behind them as the passenger in the opposition's car leaned out with a machine pistol. The salvo punched through the BMW's trunk lid and part of the back seat. A follow-up burst shattered part of the dash, spraying bits of plastic in Dane's face. A slug punched through Wexler's right shoulder. Wexler howled, slumping forward, the BMW swerving. The tires bumped the curb and the car crossed the sidewalk, smashing through a fenced-off section of blacktop. Dane jumped up with his knees on his seat, and returned fire with the Detonics .45, but none of his shots connected with the gunman.

Wexler hit the brakes. The tires screeched. Wexler crawled across the front, smearing the leather with blood. Dane jumped to the pavement as another burst of full-auto fire came his way. The shots thumped into the car. Wexler screamed again. He fell out of the car on the passenger side and crashed into Dane.

The automatic fire stopped. Dane scrambled back.

"Tommy!"

"Roll me over." Dane turned Wexler onto his back. Wexler winced, crying out. Cold wind blew from the bay, drying the sweat on Dane's face. He examined Wexler's wounds. Shoulder and chest, both bleeding heavily.

Wexler wheezed. "Steve. You gotta...gotta get to Holly."

The machine pistol started up again followed by single shots. Wexler clawed under his coat. "My gun!" Dane told him to stay put, reloaded his .45 and crouched at the back wheel. He fired twice.

Glass shattered and a sharp cry echoed but neither of the two men dropped. They returned fire. A slug whined off Wexler's bumper. Another bullet exploded the back tire. Bits of rubber and radial pelted Dane's shirt. He fired two more shots. Another scream and the gunner on the passenger side of the four-door fell. Dane dropped onto his belly, aimed under the driver's door, and fired at the other man's exposed shoes. Both feet jumped. Dane fired the last round into the door as the driver dived back behind the wheel and left a cloud of smoke going in reverse. Dane reloaded again and stood up. He triggered a line of slugs into the windshield, the glass popping with each hit but not shattering. The four-door screeched through a U-turn and knocked down part of the fence as it sped away.

"My aim is getting sloppy."

Wexler didn't respond.

Dane knelt beside his friend. "Hey." Wexler's dead eyes stared at the sky. Dane let out a breath and thumbed the eyes closed.

"I'll find her, Tommy."

Dane went over to the other body. The man's muscular build looked like many of the soldiers or mercs Dane had come across in the last decade. He patted the man's pockets. No wallet. He found a cell phone.

Dane stashed the cell phone and went back to Tommy's body. He'd have to leave his friend behind, and he couldn't drive the bloodied and bullet-scarred BMW. Escape meant running away on his own. Sirens in the distance now. Dane knelt next to Tommy's body and started going through his pants pockets but didn't find anything of value. He was about to start on the overcoat when the wailing sirens increased in volume. Blood already covered Dane's hands and coat. He turned the jacket inside out, wiped his hands on Tommy's pants, and took off running with his lips in a flat line.

Dane had never left a man behind before. Today he'd done so out of necessity. But when somebody kills a friend you have to do something about it, and Dane intended to follow that rule no matter where the trail led.

And the trail started with a woman named Holly whom Dane had never met.

Chapter Five

Dane raced across the street and around a building to Spear Street. The sirens were louder now, close to the scene. Dane ducked into an alley. He leaned against the wall, the rough brick digging into his back. He ignored it and caught his breath. His side hurt. That would fade. His friend was dead. The pain of Tommy's loss wouldn't fade, and he'd make somebody pay for that.

He leaned forward, still panting. The tan lining of his overcoat at least made it look somewhat normal as long as nobody looked too closely. When his breathing slowed, he straightened up and started walking in the general direction of the hotel. Only a few blocks.

He crossed busy Market Street, mixing with the flow of other pedestrians, and reentered the Hyatt. Nobody paid him any attention. This time, the lurching elevator didn't startle him.

Back in his room, he stripped and showered and dressed again. The dirty and bloody clothes he stuffed into a sack and carried out to a Dumpster in the alley beside the hotel. There were no identifying marks on the clothes that would lead back to him.

Dane pulled a bottle of Bulleit Bourbon from his suit-case and poured two fingers into a bathroom glass, adding a splash of tap water. He paced the floor while he drank. Nothing to go on, nowhere to start. The only clue was the dead killer's cell phone, and what could he do with that? A wise man would pull up stakes and get on the next flight out of town to anywhere. Steve Dane was wise, but he couldn't abandon Tommy twice.

He stepped onto the balcony and looked down at the street. Cars and busses were jammed together. Pedestrians covered the sidewalk and crossed the street between ve-hicles. A man on a corner with a bullhorn preached about religion, but nobody paid him any attention.

He'd never doubted the life he'd chosen before, but now the costs of such a life seemed to be adding up more and more. Dead friends, more and more violence. Perhaps it was time to hang up the guns and live a quiet life, but he had no idea what a quiet life entailed. Maybe he could have gone in a different direction, but his chosen path had seemed the only obvious escape route at the time he de-cided to go it alone.

Dane finished the bourbon, went back inside, and sat down on the bed. He wasn't going to do anything until Nina arrived. He stretched out on the bed and contem-plated the ceiling for a moment. Within a few minutes he dozed off.

The phone rang and woke him up. Dane stared at the phone. Nobody else knew he was here. He reached over and picked up. "Yes?"

"Mr. Dane?" the voice said.

"Yes," Dane said.

"My name is Gino Vicini and I'm an inspector with the San Francisco police. Do you know a Thomas Wexler?"

Dane breathed quietly. The city worked fast. If he'd had more time to search Tom's body...

"Yes. We're supposed to meet today."

"I'm sorry to tell you that Mr. Wexler has passed away. We found your name amongst Mr. Wexler's personal items. He's not from around here and we have no next-of-kin yet. I need you to come to the morgue and identify the body; would that be okay?"

That didn't make sense. "Why do I need to identify the body if you already know his name?"

"We have a few questions for you, Mr. Dane. Make this easy and come on down, okay?"

Dane paused. What about the woman Tommy had mentioned? Was there no trace of her? If so, he truly had nowhere to go and now the cops held all the cards.

"When?" Dane said.

Later, Dane's face remained still, hands warm in his pockets, as the inspector pulled the morgue drawer open. The metal track moaned. Dane looked at the wrapped body as a mist of chilled air touched his cheeks. The inspector unzipped the body bag and exposed the dead man's face.

Dane blinked. He'd seen Tommy die. The sight of him again, his eyes closed, appearing in a somewhat peaceful state, struck him like a fist. He swallowed a lump in his throat.

Dane cleared his throat. "That's Tommy."

Inspector Gino Vicini shoved the drawer closed. The gold ring on his finger twinkled from the overhead light. "Let's go talk about it."

"There's nothing to talk about." Dane turned for the door, pushed through. The fluorescent lights reflected brightness off the tiled floor and Dane squinted. The air conditioning didn't make the hall as cold as the cooler, but Dane felt a chill up his neck which irritated him. His shoes squeaked on the floor as he made a left turn and headed for the exit ahead.

The inspector caught up. "Tom Wexler had your name in his personal effects."

"You said that on the phone."

"He had information on your flight number and died about an hour after you landed. We have evidence that two people were in his BMW. Were you in the car?"

Dane reached for the exit door.

Vicini grabbed his arm. "I'm serious."

Dane twisted out of the grip and put a hand on the cold metal crash bar. "What do you want to know? Tom and I are pals from way back. It's been some time since we last saw each other so we were going to catch up. I don't know who shot him and I don't know why he was shot. No, he didn't meet me at the airport. He was supposed to. When he didn't show up, I took a cab."

"You can prove that?"

"Would I tell you a lie?"

"How did you know Mr. Wexler?"

"We were in the Army together. Maybe the Peace Corp. I forget things."

Dane pushed the door open and started down the outside steps. The bright sun made him squint, too, but the fresh air felt good, and his skin warmed under the sunlight. When his feet hit the sidewalk, the inspector called out, "I'm not through with you. I know trouble when I see it."

Dane didn't turn around. He said, "Goodbye, Inspector," and kept walking.

Chapter Six

Dane found a near-empty bar and sat in the back with a beer. He stared at a spot on the wall. So much for arriving in town using his own name. The verbal tussle would get Vicini fired up enough to look up Dane's file, and the information would tell the cop that Dane was indeed not who he seemed. A second meeting would follow, but he had an idea on how to approach that, and how to use the inspector for his own goals.

Sentimental memories were a waste of time, but he let them flow through his mind without protest. The last time he had seen Tom was at a hotel bar in Brazil, where Dane was catching some sun with Nina, and Tom was passing through on his way further south. Dane introduced him to Nina but when she excused herself from their table, Tommy leaned close.

"She's Russian."

"You noticed?"

"Where'd you meet her?"

"Casino in Montenegro," Dane said. "Both of us were checking on rumors that some of Anastasia's jewels were being sold on the black market but they were fakes. I got the girl, though."

"If history had gone any differently you two would've tried to kill each other."

"Then let's have a toast and thank the God that you don't believe in that history turned out the way it did."

Dane almost smiled and drank some beer. Revenge wouldn't make him feel better. He knew that. He'd learned that lesson the hard way many times. But accounts had to be settled. Nobody lived in a vacuum and nobody could die in one, either.

Tommy was late.

Holly Mendoza checked her watch and her phone to make sure she hadn't misread. Tommy and his friend were supposed to have arrived at 2:15. It was now 2:45. She sat in a corner in the outdoor area of a coffee shop in Union Square across from Macy's and the center plaza. A plant partially shielded her from view.

She sat there watching traffic and people...and Tommy was late. She held her coffee in her left hand while her purse, containing the usual items along with her 9mm SIG-Sauer P-239 automatic, rested on the table. The top remained unzipped for easy access to the gun should she require it. As the minutes ticked by, a gnawing fear grew in the pit of her stomach. Something had gone wrong and she had to get moving. Anywhere. When she spotted two familiar faces, she knew that the hourglass had run out. The faces belonged to thugs who had worked side-by-side with Skinner McNab. If they were here, so was he.

Holly placed her coffee on the table, reached for the mobile phone in her purse and purposely dropped it. While she leaned over to pick it up, the thugs passed the coffee shop and didn't see her. Through the corner of her eye she watched them pass. They were scanning the crowded sidewalk, trying to catch everything. She put the phone back in her purse, left the table, and started walking in the opposite direction.

Enough pedestrians crowded the sidewalk, so she didn't think about cover. They provided cover for her; at an even five and a half feet, she was smaller than most, and it was the first time she'd ever been grateful for her height deficiency. At the corner of Post, she crossed Powell and walked along the plaza to Macy's where she followed some chatty women through the front door and into the department store. She didn't want a gun fight and since she had the crowd to hide in, there was no reason not to use it. She browsed around to blend in, smiling politely at the salesgirls who offered to let her try this or that fragrance as she moved through the makeup department, and eventually found a padded bench where she sat and dialed Tom. The line went straight to voicemail. She did not leave a message. Her heart sank. What had happened? She dropped her eyes to the tiled floor.

What to do? Had they caught up with Tom? What about the friend Tom had sent for? How could she contact him? Presently she shook herself out of a daydream and cursed her carelessness. She'd been staring at the tiled floor for far too long. Leaving the bench she continued through the store, one end to the other. How long before the goons moved to another location? They had no idea where to find her...right? Did something lead them to Union Square, or did they follow a simple search pattern? She froze again, the gnawing returning to her belly. Had they made Tom talk? Was he still alive?

She found the exit leading to O'Farrell Street, walked to

the corner and turned left at Stockton, heading toward Market and the crowds there. More shops, restaurants, people, and the Powell Street BART station. She could hop a train across the bay and put miles and miles of water between her and Skinner's goons.

Again she mixed with the swarm of pedestrians, vehicle traffic congesting the street. Homeless people either stood begging, or sat on the cold sidewalk, but their signs all said the same thing. Some didn't have signs and talked out loud to nobody. Street musicians played music. As she neared Market, the valley produced by a block of buildings amplified a drummer and guitar combo as they cranked out an up-tempo number. Passing tourists stopped to listen. The drummer's dreadlocks jerked back and forth as he worked the skins. The natives strolled right by. Nothing to see, folks. A pair of Japanese tourists held up iPhones and took pictures of the combo.

Holly crossed Market. The BART station lay ahead.

She stopped cold. A young woman collided behind her. Holly apologized and let the woman go around. The woman did not curse or acknowledge Holly. She continued on her way and blocked Holly just enough for her to look at the gunman near the train entrance and consider the few options left open to her.

Leaning against the railing leading down to the underground train station, smoking a cigarette, was another of Skinner's goons. He looked at almost every face as it passed. They were everywhere!

She started to turn and—

A hand grabbed her left arm in a vice grip. She choked back a gasp. Something pointy and cold and metal touched her back through the fabric of her top. "Never stay in place for too long," Skinner McNab said in her ear.

Chapter Seven

Holly's whole body stiffened. She didn't turn her head.

"We got Tom, I'm afraid," Skinner said. "He died fighting."

Holly spat out a curse.

"Now, now, babe, no need for that. You and I are going to have a chat over in this alley, okay?"

He tugged on her arm, leading the way to the narrow alley just off the sidewalk. A bum near the alley smiled at them and said, "Spare a dollar?"

"Go to hell," Skinner said.

He shoved Holly against the hard rock wall and placed the point of his knife at her belly button. A dumpster off to the side filled the alley with a gross smell. Holly's nose twitched.

The bum loomed behind Skinner and jabbed him in the shoulder. "Hey. I don't like you talking to me like that."

Skinner didn't look back at the man. "Go away."

"You can't go around talking to people like that."

Skinner pivoted and plunged the blade into the bum's solar plexus. He shoved the man against the opposite wall.

The man's face twisted in a silent scream. Skinner pulled out the blade. The bum fell onto the ground. Skinner turned back to Holly. She'd drawn the SIG-Sauer and had the pistol leveled at Skinner's neck. As she eased back the trigger he swiped with the knife. She recoiled back to avoid the blade, lost her balance and hit the ground hard. She fired at Skinner's knees, missed, and he kicked her in the stomach. She cried out, bringing her knees up to her chest. Skinner reached for the gun. She swung as hard as she could and bashed him in the side of the head. Skinner fell to the side, rolling a bit. He stopped and jumped to his feet as Holly started running the length of the alley to the other side. Skinner shouted after her. Two shots popped and the bullets nicked her heels. She risked a look back. The thug with the cigarette had joined Skinner and was lining up another shot. Holly spun around, fired a shot of her own, and both Skinner and the gunman ducked back. Somewhere she heard people screaming.

Her pulse pounded in her head and her breath came in short gasps as she ran, clearing the alley, turning right. As she glanced around for a way to go, more thugs zeroed in. They were closing the box. If she didn't find a way out fast, she'd be trapped and as dead as Tom.

She walked fast, dodging pedestrians that were oblivious to her. No police sirens yet. It would take time before they arrived, and she couldn't count on their help. Not with a loaded gun in her purse. She passed a row of stone steps leading to the front door of a church. She ran up the steps and tried the door – locked. Terrific. Back on the sidewalk. She kept walking. The tall buildings blotted out the sun. She shivered. A harsh wind swept through the valley of stone and kicked up debris on the sidewalk that was soon trampled by the mass of people walking along with no idea of the drama playing out around them.

She looked ahead, to the side, and behind her, but so far, the goons hadn't caught up. She couldn't spot them either. Had they scattered with the shooting? Not likely, but one hoped.

She dashed across the street, dodging the stopped cars, and slipped into a Mexican restaurant. Near the front door, a woman as old as the earth cooked flour tortillas on a griddle and did not look at Holly as she entered. Nobody occupied any of the tables and the tired old woman behind the counter did not regard Holly with any enthusiasm. Holly found a back table. The smells from the kitchen would normally have been pleasing; today, not at all. The old woman from the counter, her hair tied back in a bun and wearing a gray Mumu, waddled over. Holly asked for ice water.

She put her face in her hands. Both her hands and face were sweaty, and she used a napkin to wipe off her face and rubbed her hands on her jeans. She eventually caught her breath. A sharp cramp bit at the right side of her belly.

No time to think of Tom now. That could wait. Right now she needed a plan of action and—

The ice water landed on the table with a hard thud. Holly looked up. The older woman took out her pen and pad. "What do you want?"

"Nothing right now," Holly said.

"You can't come in here and drink water."

"I need a minute, okay?"

"I'll give you a minute but you better order something. I'm not running a rest stop."

Holly mashed her teeth and stood up, cursed the woman to her face and started for the door but stopped when Skinner and another gunner entered.

"There you are," Skinner said. He and the gunman converged.

Holly shoved the old lady in front of her. The old woman huffed and screamed as she landed on the floor, knocking over a chair and almost tipping a table, forcing Skinner and the gunman to jump over her as Holly made for the back exit. She crashed through the door, into another alley, raised her gun and fired three rapid shots into the restaurant. Turning right, she ran for the mouth of the alley and halted as yet another gunman turned into it. She fired and scored a hit, the slugs punched through the man's chest. She ran at a zigzag pattern as Skinner and his partner fired at her. As she neared the mouth of the alley, she winged a shot back at them. Pedestrians screamed and scattered; Holly took the opportunity to vault into a waiting cab. Another couple had already opened the door but scattered with the rest when the shooting started. She showed the driver her gun and told him to drive. The cabbie let out a yell and she jabbed the gun against the wire mesh dividing back from front and told him to get moving. He impulsively hit the meter before he pulled into traffic, quickly accelerating.

Holly, breathless, reloaded her gun. "Just drive until I tell you to stop," she said.

"Um, hey. I don't have any money on me. You can be cool with that piece."

"I'm not going to rob you or hurt you. I need you to drive. I will pay you."

The driver said nothing more.

Holly put away the SIG and waited for her breathing to return to normal before she engaged her brain. No more Tom. No idea how to reach his friend. There was only one avenue open to her now, and it would leave her a sitting duck if they found her. If Tom's friend were able to trace her from the hideout she and Tom had shared, and she knew the clue was there because she'd personally planted it, she had to remain in one spot so he could reach her. Then they could get about the business of avenging Tom and recovering the treasure. She was putting her trust in somebody she had never met, but only because Tom had said he was trustworthy.

"You need to put on your seatbelt, miss," the driver said.

She stared at the back of his head with her mouth agape. Are you kidding? She wanted to tell him to stuff it, but decided the man was not her enemy and making him one wasn't productive. Maybe he could drive her across the bay. She scooted near the door, buckled up, and tried to relax.

Chapter Eight

Skinner stretched out in the back seat of the Lincoln Town car and dialed a number on his cell. His driver merged onto the freeway and joined the flow of traffic, heading for home base.

Joe Thorne answered on the first ring. "Did you get her?"

"She got away. We lost Hutch."

"You know where she's going, right?"

"She's tiny and moves quick but she had no idea how many eyes were on her," Skinner said. "She jumped into a cab and the team followed it to the Palace Motel. She's holed up there now."

Joe Thorne said nothing.

"I think we should go in and get her," Skinner said.

"What about the man Tom picked up at the airport?"

"What about him?"

"He'll be looking for Holly."

"So?"

"The motel is probably a rendezvous. He'll go there eventually. We can kill two birds. Plant a team at the motel and tell them to wait until he shows up."

"And if he doesn't?"

"Let's give him a couple of days. Won't hurt."

Skinner said OK and hung up. He breathed deep, let it out slow.

At the Hyatt's office center, Steve Dane scoured the internet for information on Sam Roca and antiques stolen from Iraq. When he found an article of interest, he printed it for review. Later, he made half a dozen calls to various contacts around the world to learn more. He wanted to be able to give Nina a full rundown when she arrived. After a couple of hours, he poured a drink, sat out on the deck, and did some reading as the fog rolled in. He hoped Nina was having a better time than he.

Somewhere in Germany

Nina Talikova wasn't nervous because of the job or because she was working alone. Years ago, she'd been trained by the best the Russian FSB had to offer and spent most of her field career indeed working alone. What made her stomach quiver just a little was sitting next to a bomb.

Or, rather, the briefcase full of plastic explosives on the passenger seat beside her. Despite all her years of experience, all the scrapes she'd been in, bombs still made her nervous.

In the case were wrapped stacks of $100 bills, $50,000 worth. Monopoly money. Counterfeit. Beneath that façade, the stuff that went boom.

The mall parking lot was empty except for her. Trees circled the lot, the only open spaces between them the various entry ways. Black lampposts on cement bases lit the area, casting tentacle-like shadows on the pavement. She made a circuit of the lot, stopped the car, killed the lights, engine. She cranked down the window and listened to the crickets. The crisp air felt good. In front of the mall, a large digital clock on the side of a tall tower showed 1:55 a.m. Nina had scouted the location earlier in the day, when the lot had been packed with cars, shoppers loaded down with bags. It seemed like a ghost town now.

She disliked meeting out in the open like this, but her personal discomfort meant little considering the objective. The other side would be pretty keyed up too. She certainly was and could feel her heart jumping. She took a few deep breaths and envisioned a victory in her mind. Never let them see you sweat, the commercial used to say, and Nina believed in that philosophy.

The cell phone in her pocket chirped. She answered. "I'm set."

"Ditto," said Todd McConn. "The van left the house with two men and the Loren kid. The woman and the other man are still inside."

"The van's just turning in now."

"Copy. Standing by."

A screech echoed as the white minivan jumped the curb, turned through the entrance on the other side of the lot. A brand-new van, without a mark or smudge, light from the lampposts glinting off its shiny exterior. Nina put away the phone and hopped out of the car with briefcase in hand. The van approached with bright headlights. The windows had been tinted. She set the briefcase on the ground.

The van stopped perpendicular to Nina's car, driver's side facing her. The driver powered down his window, leveled a black sawed-off shotgun. A double-barreled piece. Old school hardware. The wide mouths of the barrels looked big enough to stuff with basketballs, but Nina had a 9mm Smith & Wesson M&P Shield semi-auto strapped under her left arm that was more than a match. She didn't have to reload after only discharging two rounds, either.

The driver wore a black hood, only his eyes visible. He watched Nina without blinking, pointed the snout of the shotgun at the briefcase.

Nina picked up the case, rested it on her left palm, popped the locks. Lifting the lid, she turned the case so the driver could see the money.

The driver said, "Down."

She closed the case and set it on the ground again.

The van's side door rumbled open. Another man jumped out. He wore a hood that matched the driver's and a zipped windbreaker that stretched tight around his bulging pot belly. He carried a shiny pistol and kept the barrel on Nina as he hauled a haggard-looking male teenager with sandy blond hair out of the back. The boy looked at Nina with wide eyes. His blue jeans and T-shirt were torn, smudged with dirt.

The driver said, "Bring the case."

Nina picked up the briefcase. The driver kept her covered while the other tucked the pistol in his belt, put both arms on the boy, shoved him forward. The boy staggered past Nina, hit the ground. Nina said: "Get in the car, Andrew," and raised the case to the second gunman, who grabbed the case in his left hand, snatched his gun with his right hand, pushed the barrel into Nina's belly. "Get back." She stepped backwards with both hands waist high.

The driver withdrew his sawed-off and put the van in gear. His partner jumped in as the driver started back the way he'd come.

Andrew Loren remained on the ground his blue eyes fixed on his unknown benefactor. Must be quite a sight, Nina thought, dressed head-to-toe in black, including a long black leather coat that whipped around her ankles as she approached.

She reached down, hauled Andrew to his feet, hustled him to the passenger side of her car. She didn't need to help the boy get in.

Back behind the wheel, Nina started the engine, picked up a small remote control from where it sat on the dashboard.

"Who are you? Did my dad send you?"

"Quiet."

Nina extended a small antenna from the remote. Nina pressed a green button. The van continued rolling toward the exit. She pressed the button a second time and let out a curse.

"Andrew, get as low as you can," she said.

The van's break lights flashed and somebody inside tossed the briefcase out the window. It struck the ground, opening, the funny money flying into the air.

The reverse lights snapped on, and the vehicle screeched as the driver sped backward. Nina jumped out of her car, drawing the Smith & Wesson. The van's tires screeched again as the driver spun it around so the front faced her. Nina fired twice into the windshield, but the driver stomped the pedal and raced toward her.

Chapter Nine

She ran from the car, diving and rolling as the van tried to run her down. As she rolled up onto her back, the side door opened and Pot Belly fired, his rounds striking the ground beside her, spraying bits of asphalt into her face. She fired once, missed, fired twice. Pot Belly grunted and fell out of the van but started to get up again. The driver moved the van away from him, starting to circle it again so he could take a shot. Pot Belly raised his gun once more. Nina shot him in the head. This time he stayed on the ground.

She rolled to her feet as the van surged toward her. The driver leveled the sawed-off out the window and fired one barrel, but the pellet blast flew wide. Nina stitched three more rounds into the windscreen, but none struck the driver. The van turned away again, laying another patch of rubber. Nina slapped another magazine into her gun. As the van spun around again, the driver fired his last shell. Nina loosed three rounds and this time they connected, tearing into the driver's chest. She rolled out of the way as the van continued toward her. Getting up, she watched the van crash into the lamppost where it stopped, the engine still running.

She ran back to her car.

Andrew Loren stared at her as if he'd just been smacked in the face with a basketball.

"All in a night's work," Nina said, and made a sharp U-turn.

As they hit the street, she dialed Todd and said: "I have the boy. Hit the house."

On the freeway, she dialed another number. A man answered. He said: "Yeh—uh, yes?"

Nina didn't blame the man for being nervous. She said, "Mr. Loren. I have your son. We'll be there shortly."

The elder Loren let out some air and a "Thank God" and said: "Any problems?"

"Nope."

Loren wanted to talk to his son, so she passed the phone to Andrew. They talked for a moment, the younger man assuring his father that he was not hurt, and Nina took back the phone when they finished. She ended the connection without saying anything further to the client.

It only took an hour to drive Andrew back to his father's town home. In that time Todd McConn called back and said the remaining two kidnappers wouldn't be bothering anybody ever again.

At the town home, Nina assured Michael Loren that all was well, but the millionaire sports consultant wouldn't let her leave without a $5000 bonus check. He'd already paid Dane $10,000 in advance three days earlier, and Nina refused the bonus, but the grateful father insisted, so she took the check. After all, what the hell.

From sexy gunslinger to typical tourist in less than twelve hours, Nina thought. Instead of head-to-toe black, she now wore a comfortable T-shirt and jeans, her long hair tied back, with stray strands dangling alongside either side of her face. Todd McConn walked beside her, his usual cowboy boots thunk-thunking on the tiled floor.

They moved through the flood of travelers at Berlin's Tegel International Airport. Nobody paid them any attention, and Nina appreciated the anonymity. Too often she felt the flash and dash preferred by Steve put an unnecessary spotlight on them. The lifestyle was something he enjoyed while she favored discretion. But he was a charmer and it was hard to argue about it.

"Here's my gate," McConn said, stopping and turning to her. "Tell Steve I'm at loose ends the next few weeks so if he needs help again, don't forget me."

She laughed and hugged him. "You'll have your pay by the end of the week," she added.

"I've made more off Steve more than anybody else the last few months. See you next time."

She said goodbye and moved on with a sigh. She had a long flight ahead and hated to make the trip alone. Her eyes darted left and right, her neck and shoulders tightening, the usual fight-or-flight she felt whenever she was alone. A lithe feral cat. But there was nobody here to harm her. She knew that. She also knew that could change and she had to be ready. She wanted to blame too many years of field work but that would have been a lie. She could trace her anxiety to one freezing Moscow night under the Zhivopisny Bridge when she was twenty-three years old, fighting the chill off the Moskva River, while men with guns hunted for her.

Her nightmares hadn't helped either.

But both items were related.

She had not wanted Steve to go to San Francisco, but also didn't want to insist that he stay, especially with Mc-Conn present. It would have shown weakness, and she wasn't going to do that no matter how she felt. It wasn't that she couldn't complete the Loren job, but she needed Steve's calming presence. His charm. Co-dependent? Maybe not textbook, but probably, and she wasn't interested in pursuing the idea further.

She found her gate and browsed a newsstand and the awful women's magazines on display just long enough to talk herself into a vodka on the rocks at the adjoining bar. She placed her carry-on on the counter and ordered her drink. Two businessmen at a table behind her gave her the eye. The bartender brought her drink and she took a long sip. As the alcohol burned down her throat and warmed her stomach, she started feeling better.

Across the terminal, through the wide side windows, she watched planes come and go. This wasn't the first time she had visited the airport. It also wasn't the first time a member of her family had set foot on the property. Her grandfather, an undercover KGB agent in 1948, once told her about his observation of the Berlin airlift at that very location.

Post-WW2, 1948 to '49, the first major engagement of the Cold War. Her grandpa had been working in the shadows with the occupation forces when the Soviet Union blocked the Western Allies' railway, road, and canal access to the sectors of Berlin under Allied control. The Russians wanted the western governments to allow the Soviet zone to supply Berlin with food, fuel, and necessities, which would have given the Russians near total control over the entire city.

He had told her that it was a dangerous time, with tension high between the East and West, but he, and others, knew what the Americans feared to admit: the Soviets outnumbered the Allied military forces, which had downsized after the war. It would not have been much of a fight until the atomic weapons were used.

The Western powers responded with the Berlin Airlift to carry supplies to the citizens in West Berlin. Over 200,000 flights in one year delivering more supplies than the Russians could. It took the fight out of the Soviets, who hadn't thought the effort would succeed. The event ultimately resulted in the formation of the two separate German states, and later the Berlin Wall.

A dangerous time, indeed.

She'd been 13 when the wall came down.

Nina wondered what grandpa would think about the time she was living in. It seemed just as dangerous, if not more so, and she wished she had the perspective of age to truly round out her opinion. The Cold War might have been long over, but plenty of conflict remained in the world, and at any moment hostilities somewhere could lead to global chaos.

She finished her drink and ordered another.

She had warm memories of her grandfather, that mostly silent man who had trouble showing affection, but always communicated his love for young Nina by pulling on her earlobe while she sat at her grandmother's kitchen table coloring.

She did not, however, have warm feelings for her father, and shivered at the vision of the man in black present in her dreams.

Her father.

The man she least wanted to see ever again, but destiny

was pulling her into his orbit. She and Dane had solved the mystery of his father, and now it was her turn. She needed to face the inevitable confrontation with the same bravery Steve had shown.

But she wondered if that were possible.

The gate attendant announced the boarding of her flight. She downed the rest of her drink in two quick gulps and grabbed her carry-on.

Chapter Ten

The two businessmen wound up sitting next to her on the plane. Nina dreaded their presence. Their shop talk would probably last the whole flight.

When the in-flight movie began, she used the opportunity to sit back and take a nap. Nothing disturbed her sleep. This time.

A connecting flight in New York finally brought her to San Francisco and she found Steve Dane waiting for her in the baggage claim area. She half ran toward him and he scooped her up, squeezing her tight.

"How was Germany?" he said.

"Almost a bust," she said. "The you-know-what didn't work and I had to shoot my way out."

The baggage carousel began its rotation, luggage sliding up the conveyer belt and sliding down the ramp.

"The you-know-what was guaranteed; what happened?"

"I pressed the button and nothing happened. Totally fizzled. It must have done something because the goons tossed it out the window. Next time let's just build a bomb from instructions on the Internet."

"Did you get paid?"

"Of course I got paid, darling."

Dane laughed, put his arm around her and squeezed.

Nina responded to Dane's partial update with: "You're here one day and you're already causing trouble."

"At least I'm not bored."

He rolled over, Nina moving off his back, her long black hair tickled his cold skin. He focused his eyes on the ceiling. The dark-eyed naked woman beside him, almost covered by the white sheet, traced a finger along the fire-scarred puckered flesh of his right arm.

Nina put her head on his chest. "Did I ever meet Tom?"

"Brazil."

"Right. He had a full head of hair. Thick, sloppy brown hair."

"Yes."

"Made you jealous?" she said.

"Of course not."

Dane smiled and moved his hand along her back to the scar on her right side. He rested his hand there. Their mutual scars represented only a fraction of what they shared.

"Is that cop going to bother you?" Nina said.

"No. By the time we're done here he will be my best friend."

"Well. All this exercise has made me hungry."

"Breathing makes you hungry."

They showered and dressed again, and Dane ordered room service.

"Help me make the bed," Nina said.

Dane put the phone down. "What for?"

"It's still early and if they see it like this they'll know we've been fooling around."

"Nina, it's a whole separate room."

"Come on, help me."

Dane knew better than to argue.

Dinner arrived and they sat with the window open, but no street sounds penetrated the upper-floor room. Only the cool evening air filtered through the screen. They were high enough that the sewer smell couldn't reach them. Dane took large bites of his salmon-and-cream-sauce dinner, mixing the fish and vegetables with the garlic mashed potatoes that accompanied the fish. Nina took small bites of her steak. Her high Slavic cheekbones and sunken cheeks, along with her wiry but muscled frame, gave her the look of somebody who was always starving. Dane cleaned his plate and sat back. Nina continued chewing with little noise. He watched her. She kept her eyes on the plate. He knew about her dreams, although she hadn't outright said anything about them. It was the only thing that explained why she'd been tossing and turning of late and getting up for extended periods of time. She'd talk about it when she was ready. He knew better, after their last adventure, to press for details before she wanted to talk.

She said, "Tell me what you've learned so far."

Dane retrieved the printouts from the computer and notes from his telephone conversations. Nina scooted closer as Dane showed her the material.

"Antiques looted from Iraq," Dane said. "It started almost as soon as the US invaded and became progressively worse, and all these years later it's become a hot-button topic among the diplomats. Iraq says US forces did nothing to protect the artifacts and let smugglers loot whatever wasn't nailed down."

"Why would the Americans do that?"

"Can't blame the troops," Dane said. "They probably

had orders to stand-down, or certainly a lack of manpower to deal with the looters."

"How much is it all worth?"

"A ton of money, though Iraq claims it's all priceless. They're right. This is the legacy of their country we're talking about. I don't care what you think of them now, but history is history and it should be preserved. But it all looks good in a private collection, and there are plenty willing to risk having it."

He paused. He couldn't leave out the other details Tom Wexler had mentioned, and he carefully explained the human trafficking connection, and the goal of using the funds generated by the sale of the antiques to fund the as-yet-unknown syndicate.

Nina said nothing, but her expression changed. She didn't look upset, however. She looked scared.

"What are you thinking?" he said.

"Never mind. Keep talking."

Dane showed her a picture of Sam Roca, in full-military dress, the man Wexler had said was in charge of the recovery operation and leading the fight against the trafficking syndicate. The picture showed Roca testifying before Congress.

"It's the only photo of him I could find," he said. "He's giving a report on a friendly fire incident. Roca retired a few years ago and learned that Iraq was offering very generous rewards for the return of their artifacts, so he formed an organization of bounty hunters and mercenaries to scour the world looking for stuff, and he managed to turn in a lot.

"According to Tom, the latest cache they were tracking is hidden here in the US."

"Did he infiltrate the smugglers?"

"Must have. He told me he didn't get deep enough to

find out who was in charge, but he did discover Thorne and Skinner as the muscle working on the outside."

"And this map is now in pieces."

"Uh-huh."

"Who are the people Roca sent the pieces to?"

Dane showed her another printout. "They're his financiers. Meyer, Grimmer, Nash. Grimmer is retired but the other two are still working. They finance the search and recovery for a portion of the reward."

"And we have no idea where they are."

"Tom's girlfriend knows. I think one of them is either in San Francisco, or nearby."

"But we have no idea where Tom's girlfriend is. We don't even know if she's still alive."

"Yup."

"And one of them may have betrayed the whole operation."

"Uh-huh," Dane said.

"This is going to be fun," Nina said.

Dane grinned. He left the table and retrieved the captured cell phone from the top of the dresser. He sat down again and scrolled through the previous call list. Three numbers, all identical. Dane dialed. Nina leaned forward to watch him. Dane winked at her. She smiled back. He waited.

Chapter Eleven

A man answered the other line. "Who is this?" The voice sounded like two pieces of sandpaper rubbing together. Dane frowned. He knew the voice.

Dane said, "You weren't expecting a call from this phone, were you? Probably because the previous owner is dead."

"Hello, Dane."

"Hello, Skinner."

"I knew we'd face each other again someday."

"Your guys tried their best but you forgot who the best is. I'll be shooting some more of your guys very soon. Eventually I'll get to you. You'll wish that grenade had got you."

The other man paused, then let out a laugh. "Tom's aim was a little off. And you're still as arrogant as ever. We're not what we used to be. You taught us a lot, but we figured out even more for ourselves."

"People like you and Joe don't change, Skinner. You just become worse."

"Be seeing you, Dane. I promise we'll surprise you."

The other man hung up. A chill raced up Dane's spine. He took the phone from his ear and stared at the screen a moment.

"Don't tell me," Nina said, "let me guess. You reached the dead killer's uncle and he's very confused right now."

Dane put the phone on the table. "Nope," he said. "That was Skinner."

"You think that cop will cooperate? Do you even think he knows where to find this mysterious Holly?"

"He's traced the dead gunman by now. He'll know something more is happening than just a simple murder."

"Do you promise lots of gunfire and explosions and intrigue and nail-biting suspense?"

"Sure."

"Do you swear you'll vanquish the villains, recover all the treasure, destroy the smugglers, and at the end run off with your sexy heroine?"

"I'm sure there will be plenty of sexy heroines to choose from."

She folded her arms and gave him a death stare.

"Dear, have I ever let you down?"

She raised an eyebrow.

"Don't answer that," he said.

Inspector Gino Vicini of the San Francisco Police Department, rocking back in his creaky chair, rolled an unlit Dutch Masters cigar between his thumb and index finger while he read the bright computer screen on his desk. He had read the e-mail three times, letting his mind absorb the words and mix with the other information he had in the file folder on his lap.

The subject: Stephen Richard Dane.

The e-mail had come from the Paris headquarters of Interpol, addressed to the chief of inspectors. The chief, knowing that Vicini had interviewed Dane, forwarded the note to him. Interpol wanted San Francisco Police to be aware of Dane's suspected involvement in numerous criminal activities, including grand larceny and murder. Interpol added that Dane could be in San Francisco as part of a criminal conspiracy posing a great threat to public safety, and that they should make the effort to detain him for questioning.

Interpol's note did not match the image of Dane formed by the information in the folder.

Born and raised in the Midwest. Short college career. Longer military career with the Marines and free-lance work with private paramilitary contract companies after an honorable discharge. But the last few years were sketchy, with rumored CIA and mercenary activity. Dane was known to live overseas in Austria, a villa in Vienna. Very little else was known of his activities or his employment.

But he hadn't worn rags to the morgue.

Vicini's father had always told him that somebody with money who had no means of earning that money had to be a criminal.

Vicini's experience told him he did not have the required amount of information to make such a decision, despite what his father would have said.

Gino Vicini was a third-generation cop. Both grandfathers had been patrolmen. His father joined the force too but broke the mould later when he became a city prosecutor. Vicini himself had not always been sure of joining the force, but his dad arranged for him to ride on patrol with a variety of officers, young bucks and crusty vets. The bug bit and Vicini had never looked back. As soon as he turned twenty-one, he took the department's entry exam. And failed.

Vicini would fail three more times before finally achieving a passing grade. He was the first in the family to make the rank of inspector. He was also the only one in the family to have a tattoo. A dedicated Catholic, Vicini had in nomine patris (in the name of the father) inked into his left arm.

"Watcha reading?"

Vicini put down the cigar, sat up, the chair making a squeal. His partner, Inspector Second Grade Jack Wade, dropped into the seat on the opposite side of Vicini's desk. Their two desks were pressed together. They occupied a small corner of the squad room on an upper floor of police headquarters. The mess on Wade's desk spilled across the border onto Vicini's clean desktop, and Wade picked at some of the invading papers and moved them to another pile.

Vicini said, "File on Dane," and explained the Interpol letter.

"Any specifics?" Wade said.

Vicini scrolled through the attachment which Interpol had included with the note.

"Dane's a suspect in the murder of an African diamond miner five years ago," Vicini said. "Apparently his paramilitary outfit was working for the guy, there was some sort of falling out, and the dude ended up face down in the desert with his hands tied behind his back and a bullet in his head."

"Maybe Dane ripped the guy off?"

"Who knows? The rest of this is Interpol speculating about Dane's involvement in other cases, lots of thefts and murders, but there's always a bigger fish left to take the fall and they admit Dane has exposed several syndicates they'd been unaware of."

"Hmmmm."

"I looked up the diamond miner, guy named Phillip Xavier. After he died, the South African police discovered he wasn't only running the diamond mine but also a drug smuggling trafficking operation. They busted a handful of his associates."

"Maybe Dane did the world a favor. But murder is murder."

"I think he was with Wexler," Vicini said.

"Sounds like we need another interview."

"Uh-huh." Vicini tapped his upper lip. "But maybe we can use him to our advantage."

"How do you mean?"

"You saw the report on the dead guy, right?"

"Wexler?"

"The other one."

"Sure. Hired gun with east coast mob connections."

"It confirms the rumors we heard last week," the inspector said. "If Wexler asked Dane to come out and help him because he was mixed up with this east coast guy somehow, but got shot before they talked, how much do you want to bet Dane will look into this on his own?"

"We can't have them blasting each other all over the city," Wade said.

"I agree. But until something happens, we have nothing to go on except rumors of east coast gunmen entering the city for a purpose our informants don't know, and two dead guys in the morgue who may be connected to that purpose. Where does that leave us? Nowhere. Let's give Dane a little space and see what he does."

"One week. Then we bring him in."

"If I'm right we'll need less than a week."

Wade's cell phone rang. He glanced at it, muted the

ring, returned the phone to his pocket.

"The card club?" Vicini said.

"Forget it."

"How much do you owe now?"

"I said don't worry about it."

Another telephone rang across the room. The secretary answered and transferred the call to Vicini.

"Inspector," the caller said, "this is Steve Dane. We didn't start off very well. I'd like to buy you a cup of coffee and explain a few things. Does tomorrow morning work for you?"

Vicini said the only word that immediately came to mind. "Sure."

Chapter Twelve

Nina woke up. She felt for Dane but his side of the bed was empty. Her heart jumped. Then she smelled cigar smoke. The clock on the night stand showed 2:45 a.m. Rising, she threw on a robe and wandered out to the deck where she found Dane, with his clothes on, leaning against the rail puffing on one of his cigars, and staring into the night.

She opened the sliding door. He turned.

"What's the matter?" she said.

"It'll pass."

"Come on, Steve."

He turned back. "It's not important."

"Tell me." She moved up beside him. The night chill raced up her neck. "Thorne and Skinner?"

"Uh-huh." He exhaled smoke. "We met in Afghanistan. I was doing a contract and they were soldiers or Marines; I forget which. Their time was almost up and they didn't want to go back home so I told them to look me up when they were discharged, and I got them a spot on the 30-30 team."

"The look on your face tells me there's a whole lot more to the story."

"I don't seem to pick the best people to work with."

Nina did not reply. Dane let some silence pass.

"What else?" Nina said.

The 30-30 Battalion, Dane explained, after their engagement with the US government ended, moved on to other conflicts, but Dane was already regretting his decision to bring Thorne and McNab on board. They were rowdy and, undisciplined operators who enjoyed the fighting a little too much.

The group was working a contract in Mexico, hired by a pair of Mexican Army generals who wanted to take on drug traffickers in a way their government wouldn't allow, when the pair finally crossed the line.

As usual the problem started in a bar. Thorne and McNab, always eager for a drink, were three pints ahead of Dane and some of the other team members when they spotted a woman they fancied. They tried to hit on her, but she blew them off. When they persisted, the woman's husband told them to go away, and McNab stabbed the man. Thorne grabbed the woman and they shoved her out the alley door. Dane bolted from his table while his teammates and others tended to the wounded husband. When he reached the alley, the woman was screaming. Thorne held her arms back while McNab worked on her clothes with his bloody knife, slicing open the front of her dress.

Dane took out his .45 fired a trio of rounds at McNab's feet.

Skinner jumped back. Thorne let the woman go, reaching for his own sidearm, but the smoking black muzzle of the .45 stopped him. The woman fell against the wall, clutching her torn dress, crying loudly.

Dane held his weapon steady on the two men. They ran off once the gathering crowd attracted police. Dane put away his gun and took care of the woman.

Thorne and McNab returned to the unit's headquarters long enough to grab their gear and split.

"They hate you for interrupting?" Nina said.

"More than that," Dane said. "They hate anybody with authority. I led the team, so we clashed often."

"And you're afraid, just like with Sean McFadden a while ago, that you'll have to kill them."

"They'd deserve it. McFadden could have been different."

"We'll get through this," Nina said. "We always do."

She ran her nails down his back and returned to bed.

Dane arrived first and stood near the door. The Starbucks wasn't crowded. The music over the ceiling speakers wasn't the typical "easy listening" that Starbucks normally insisted on playing, but a Rod Stewart tune. Dane smiled. His mother had been a huge fan. After she passed away, Dane had found a box full of Stewart CDs in her collection.

Dane scanned the available tables, some littered with discarded sections of newspapers. He did not look forward to sitting down. If this place was like every other Starbucks in the continental United States, the chairs would wobble because of a short leg. Never failed. But business was business and he could suffer for business.

A middle-aged man in a rumpled suit entered, did not look at Dane, and ordered at the counter. Dane fingered him for Vicini's partner. He'd have expected no less. Only a dummy went to a meeting without back-up.

Nina, who had arrived ten minutes earlier, occupied a center table with a pistol in her purse. She sat with her face in a book and a latte before her, wearing a long blue dress. She sat with crossed legs, and on one exposed ankle a gold chain dangled. She had slipped off her sandals, which lay under the table.

Dane carried no weapon. He had no desire to insult Vicini's intelligence. The inspector, like many cops, would know at half a glance whether or not he was packing.

When Vicini entered, Dane stepped forward with an outstretched hand.

"Inspector."

Vicini stopped short.

A few minutes before, Vicini pulled the unmarked car to the curb and said to Wade: "Go in first. I'll follow in a minute."

"You're not going to open up right away, are you?"

"Give me a little credit, Jack. I'll let him spin his wheels a bit before I say anything."

"See ya."

Wade exited the car and entered the Starbucks. Vicini tapped his fingers on the steering wheel, shifting a little in the worn seat, the padding of which had gone flat years ago. He watched a bus rumble by. A few passersby glanced inside the car, but Vicini did not acknowledge them.

He wanted Wade to go in first to establish some cover for him should things go south, but he also had no idea about how to approach the conversation. He recognized something in Dane, a hint in his posture that said he was capable of everything Interpol had described. He did not want to underestimate him as a potential opponent. He also knew that Dane would be too smart for a "tough cop" ploy, so he decided the best way to get the dialogue going would be to play it cool and let the other man start talking.

Chapter Thirteen

Presently Vicini stepped inside the coffee bar and came face-to-face with Dane's offered hand.

"Inspector."

Vicini regarded Dane for a moment. He wore an outfit similar to his attire at the morgue, obviously brand name or custom designs, perfectly pressed. Vicini had nothing in his closet that could match it, and his own rumpled jeans and untucked cowboy shirt made a sharp contrast between them. Vicini shook hands. He stepped ahead of Dane and ordered first. Green tea. Dane ordered the same.

They carried their cups to a corner table. Vicini sat with his back to the wall. The chair wobbled a little. Vicini figured Dane had a partner somewhere. A quick glance eliminated newspaper-reading Wade, and Vicini spotted a woman reading a book and sipping a latte. Black hair tied back, long blue dress, crossed legs exposed under the table. He saw one ankle had a chain on it. The big purse on the table could have contained a handgun, but the woman wore no shoes. The sandals on the floor were not made for combat.

Maybe Dane had come alone.

If so, he had more stones than Vicini thought. Or perhaps he was wrong, and Dane wasn't a potential enemy at all.

Dane angled back while Vicini sat forward, elbows on the table. He wanted to be in Dane's space, but the other man wasn't allowing that.

Dane said, "Nice tattoo."

Vicini's left sleeve was back far enough to expose the ink.

"In the name of the father," Dane translated.

"You read Latin?"

"I read a lot of things. Catholic?"

"Of course. You?"

"No. But speaking of reading, I'm sure you've read all about me."

"Uh-huh."

"Hear from my friends at Interpol? Fill your head with questions?"

"A few."

"Like what?"

Vicini sipped his tea. "Straight up, pal. What's your deal? I don't figure you for a bad guy, yet I don't think you're totally on the side of the angels."

"You're probably referring to a certain incident in South Africa, aren't you?"

"Go with that."

"Inspector," Dane said, "we can help each other, so I'm going to tell you part of my life story. It should answer your questions."

"Better not bore me."

Dane laughed. "On that South African job, I ran the 30-30 Battalion. We were a ragtag bunch of mercenary misfits from the US, England, and Australia. The job was to protect a diamond mine from bandits who also preyed on nearby villages, raping and killing and all that. One night the bandits carried out a very brutal attack against one village and the boys and I decided we had to balance the scales."

"And?"

"Simple," Dane said. "We left our posts one night and raided the bandits' camp. We killed everybody. The terror stopped."

"Uh-huh."

"We had, for a moment, stopped working for money and fought for a cause. It was the kind of event that makes a man reconsider his lifestyle."

"That's a bunch of muck."

"How so?"

"The dead mine owner. Xavier."

"If you read that far you know better than to lose any sleep over his demise. He was running cocaine on the side. With him out of the way, I formed a partnership with some other guys, and they run the mine while I hold controlling interest."

"That's where your money comes from?"

"Yup."

"All right. You're a retired merc, if that's the right word, and you still engage in questionable activities and have a buddy in the morgue that we think is dirty. And now you're making nice with me?"

"Certain things about me may be questionable," Dane said, "but they are not your concern. These activities allow me to live my life on my terms."

"I don't want your questionable activities in my city."

"Let me ask you this," Dane said. "Do you have everything you want?"

"Hardly."

"You have everything you need, right?"

Vicini nodded. "Sure."

"What would you do if you had everything you wanted, only to realize you then had nothing at all?"

"Come on, Dane."

"I'm being serious. Consider it a moment. Why are you a cop?"

Vicini blinked. "Family tradition."

"Was it what you wanted?"

"Not at first, but later it was."

"Why do you stay with it?"

"In five more years, I can retire and get a pension and a cushy corporate security job."

"No, you won't quit until they carry you out. You want to leave behind something on this earth more tangible than a carbon footprint. For you the cause is the law."

"How does that apply to you? What's your cause?"

"I do what you can't."

"Don't tell me you're interested in justice."

"I'm very much interested in justice, but not the kind you deal with."

Vicini drank some tea. "I think I get the idea. You run around the world as a rogue operative in gentleman's clothes, righting wrongs and looking out for the little guy, right?"

"I like that, but without the sarcasm. I'm a rogue gentleman." Dane smiled. "Wait until I tell my lady friend about that."

"I'm not here to feed your ego," the inspector said.

Dane kept smiling. "Have I answered your questions?"

"One more," the inspector said. "You took a big risk meeting me. I could have sacked you and turned you over to Interpol."

"But you didn't. That means you have another plan for me."

Vicini swallowed some tea.

"Gotcha, didn't I?" Dane said.

"Tell me about Wexler. What did he want?"

"Wish I knew," Dane said. "He called me a few days ago while I was in Germany. All he said was that he needed help."

"You didn't ask why?"

"Do you make a pal explain if he asks for help?"

"That again. Was he in Africa with you?"

"He was in other places with me. Now you tell one."

"We don't have anything on Wexler other than a hotel room in the Tenderloin that was empty when my partner and I checked it out," Vicini said. "The other man who was also shot is connected to something, but we don't know what yet."

"What are the rumors?"

Vicini pressed his lips together. "Everything in my head says don't trust you but my gut doesn't agree."

"It's nice to make your gut's acquaintance."

Vicini leaned back. Dane's eyes shifted to the wrapped cigar sticking out of Vicini's shirt pocket.

"What do you smoke?"

"Huh? Oh, Dutch Masters. El cheapos. I can't afford the good stuff with a daughter in college."

Dane took a plastic tube from inside his coat, opened it, and showed Vicini the cigar inside. "La Galera," he said. "This is a good smoke. Made in the Dominican Republic." Dane closed the tube and handed it across the table. "If you like it, I'll send you a box."

Vicini eyed the tube but made no move to take it.

"Don't insult me, Inspector."

Vicini stowed the tube in the same pocket as the other stogie.

Dane said, "You were saying?"

"The other man who died with Wexler has connections to the east coast mob. Over the last two weeks a bunch of shooters like him have come into the city but we have no idea what they're here for. Our informants are clueless. If they killed your friend, chances are his call for help involved them."

"I see."

"I suppose you're gonna poke around?"

"Sure. Call me a confidential informant if that helps you sleep tonight."

"I guess I've had worse informants."

"But I need somewhere to start," Dane said. "Where did Tom flop?"

Vicini rattled off a downtown address. "I think it was set aside as a place to hide if he needed it. You won't find any clues there."

"We'll see." Dane thanked the inspector, pushed back his chair, and stood up. "Enjoy that stogie." He shook the inspector's hand again, turned and went out.

Vicini watched the woman. She did not move, did not look up from her book. Maybe he had guessed wrong. He downed the rest of his tea, nodded to Wade, and the two cops hit the street.

"Did we learn anything?" Wade said as Vicini drove away.

"Not sure," Vicini said. "I want to say we have Dane on a leash, but my gut says it's the other way around."

Chapter Fourteen

Dane waited in an alley down the block, where Nina had parked her car. Presently she approached, the skirt of her blue dress flapping around her legs, holding the big purse close to her body, and they reviewed the conversation as she drove.

Dane directed her to the address Vicini had provided, and they found the dirty brick building with its paint fading and peeling trim right where the inspector said it would be. Curbside parking was full, so Dane jumped out and told Nina to circle the block.

The vestibule needed new paint; a stray cat, hunkered in a corner, played with a flake of paint he'd either clawed off the wall or found already waiting for him. Dane wished him a happy meal, or whatever it was, and turned down a darkened hallway to a door marked Super. Strange goo decorated the door. Dane kicked a few times. The chain finally rattled, and the door squeaked open. A thin man stuck his small head out.

"What?" he said.

"Let me up to Tom Wexler's room."

"Who?"

"Tom Wexler. Tenant here."

"Who are you?"

"Police."

The thin man didn't say anything a moment, his dull eyes studying Dane's face, and Dane figured he'd ask for official ID. He had a plan for that, but the man said: "Wait a sec."

After a moment the thin man returned carrying a ring of keys. His grease-stained T-shirt smelled like a double cheeseburger and spots of paint dotted his jeans. Dane followed him back to the vestibule, where the cat was licking a paw, and through another door to the stairwell, a breeding ground for foul odor.

"Ever hear of light bulbs and Clorox?" Dane said.

"Talk to the owner."

"Your parents?"

"Just my mother."

"You tell her to fix this place," Dane said, "or I'll have the housing authority close you down."

"There's a hundred bucks waiting for you downstairs."

"Is that a bribe?"

He had no answer.

"Skinny guy like you wouldn't last long in prison," Dane said. "Keep that in mind." Dane kept a smile to himself.

The thin man pushed open a door at the third-floor landing. They went down a hallway to apartment 316. Crime scene tape was across the door. Dane reached out and pulled the tape down.

The skinny man fumbled with the keys. "How long?" he said.

"Open it."

He unlocked the door, gave it a push, stepped back.

Dane said, "Get lost."

A short entryway led to a hallway; at one end a bedroom/bathroom, at the other kitchen/living room. Dane moved up and down the hall, checking each room. Frayed carpet, cracked walls, the bathroom a growing science project. The place wasn't Tom's style at all, but it made a good crash pad if the primary hideout became compromised. Vicini had been right in his summation of the place.

Dane went to the living room and started looking for hiding places. He poked through the furniture, sorted through cupboards in the kitchen, and crawled on hands and knees on the carpet looking for any spots that had been sliced. He discovered such a slice near a corner. He lifted the section and found a folded slip of paper with no writing on it but contained within the fold was a motel key.

Vicini had been wrong about the clues. He hadn't known where to look and wouldn't recognize the key as anything other than clutter.

Dane risked a broken neck going back down the stairs but made it back to the vestibule without a tumble. He kicked on the super's door again, told the kid to lock up. He gave the cat a goodbye pat on the way out. The cat meowed and stuck to Dane's heel but took off running in the opposite direction as soon as Dane reached the sidewalk.

Nina pulled up a moment later. Dane climbed back into the car and she stepped on the accelerator.

"Success?" she said.

Dane held up the motel key. "Maybe this is where the girl is staying."

"If she's still here at all," Nina said.

"We're being followed," Nina said.

"The second appearance of the ungodly," Dane said, and reached under the seat for the Detonics Scoremaster.

"Not sure we can lose them in this traffic."

"Try. I don't want another public battle."

Dane held the gun in his lap as Nina began shoving the little Ford Fiesta through openings in other lanes, working the clutch and gear lever in quick succession. Dane braced his feet on the floor to keep from shifting around in the seat. She checked the rearview as a traffic light forced her to stop. A cargo truck sat in front of them, the drone of its engine audible through the shell of the car.

"They're trying to get closer," she said.

"What car?" Dane turned around in his seat.

"Blue Dodge."

"I see it."

The blue sedan was stuck between lanes, at an angle, as the driver tried to squeeze between two other vehicles. The light changed and Nina drove forward. She turned left, pressed the accelerator, slowing for construction that blocked part of a lane. She swerved, cutting off a minivan, looked back.

"We're about to be out-horsepowered," she said.

"You couldn't have rented a more powerful car?"

"This was the only one with a stick."

Nina changed gears and swerved right. After a few blocks they left downtown and entered a residential area. Dane watched the blue Dodge speed toward them. Nina stomped the brakes and veered into the parking lot of a small but empty playground. Dane noted the homes nearby. Not the best place for a fight, but they had to make a stand before the crew in the Dodge overtook them and fired first.

She and Dane bolted from the Ford, Dane banging his knee against the door as it swung back at him. The Dodge screeched to a halt behind them. Dane dropped behind a concrete barrier separating the sandy playground from a walkway. Nina dropped flat in the sand near the slide as two men with submachine guns exited the Dodge.

Chapter Fifteen

Nina fired first. She hit one gunner low and as he lurched forward, not falling, he sprayed a burst of fire her way. The slide and jungle gym whined with bullet hits.

Dane, bracing his gun on the wall, tracked the second gunman who was still behind the driver's door. The shooter moved for cover and Dane fired. The shot hit the man in a leg. As he fell, he triggered return fire that split the air overhead.

Nina fired twice as her target triggered another burst. Her rounds punched through the man's chest and he dropped.

Dane jumped up, shoes scraping the sandy concrete, and ran to the other gunner, who was using a balance beam for support as he tried to gain his feet. He swung his weapon toward Dane. The gunner grimaced and tightened on the trigger. Dane fired once and the gunner's head jerked back.

Nina had already returned to the Ford. She let in the clutch as Dane rejoined her. He slammed the door as she swung around the Dodge and peeled off into the street.

Dane stowed the smoking Detonics .45 back under his seat. He wiped sweat from his face, his palm leaving a patch of sand on his cheek and forehead. He wiped the sand off with the back of his wrist.

Nina drove straight, and fast. Traffic through the neighborhood was thin enough that it appeared they'd slipped away. She turned through another section of homes, finally emerging on another busy street. She melted into the traffic flow. Dane opened the glove box and took out a GPS unit, using the name on the motel key, he searched for the location and the computerized voice told them where to go.

"Technology isn't so bad, is it?" Dane said.

Nina brushed at the front of her dress. "I got sand all over my clothes. In my toes, too. Damn sandals."

They found the motel and waited until nighttime. A single light burned in front of the Palace Motel's main office, which faced the street.

Nina made a circle of the parking lot, noting the other cars scattered about. Parking the Fiesta in the center of the lot, front toward street, she shut off the motor and cracked the window. Traffic from a nearby overpass filled the air with a sound like rushing wind.

"Which room?" she said.

Dane looked at the key. "Number four."

Dane slapped a fresh mag into his gun and stuffed two more magazines into a jacket pocket. He and Nina left the car and approached the door to Number 4. He slipped the key into the lock.

A curse caught in his throat as the door opened and a small feminine hand pushed out the snout of an automatic. Dane clamped his left hand on the barrel, twisting hard, shoving the door inward, yanking the gun outward.

The woman behind the door yelped, tumbled to the floor. Dane moved inside with one big step, kicked the door shut, flicked the light switch.

The petite olive-skinned brunette, fully dressed, with laced-up Nikes, made a squeaking noise as she scooted across the brown carpet, bumped the rumpled single bed. She ran a hand through her hair.

The woman—with dark circles around her eyes—didn't scream. Her eyes narrowed at Dane. Dane unloaded the gun and tossed it on the bed.

"Miss Holly, I presume," Dane said. She didn't blink. "My name is Steve Dane. This is Nina Talikova. Tom sent for me. You left the key for us to find. Good thinking."

The woman moved her eyes up and down his body, focused on his face.

An engine rumbled outside. Doors opened. Male voices. The click-clack of weapons. Nina looked out the window. "Get down!" Dane rushed toward Holly as the chatter of submachine guns filled the air.

Hot slugs shattered the window and ripped through the door, wood chips and plaster flying every which way. Holly screamed and squirmed beneath Dane. The gunfire stopped.

"Up, up, up!" Dane said, rising, Holly making a beeline for the bathroom. Nina ran past him. He scrambled after her. Nina and Holly stood by the tub, Holly breathing hard. He yelled for Nina to get out through the window above the tub. The front door crashed open. Dane leaned out and fired at the cluster of gunmen entering the room. The two men in front screamed, fell. The remaining four retreated. Dane took careful aim and fired a slug into the back of one. The gunman hit the ground hard, his weapon clattering away. Nina screamed: "Let's go!"

Dane reloaded while Nina shimmied out the window, followed by Holly. He put the gun away and grasped the windowsill and hauled through head and shoulders first. Gravity took over and he put his arms out to break the fall and tumbled onto his back. The dirt was soft, mixed with sharp rocks.

He rose and took out his gun, tried to listen for any sounds, but the gunfire had partially deafened him. The gunmen would assume they'd escape through the window and split up to circle around the back.

"That way," Dane told Nina. She started around the other side of the building. Dane held out his hand to Holly; she took it. They moved to the left, staying close to the wall.

They reached an opening in the wall, the point at which the first building stopped, and a second building sat at a 90-degree angle. Dane stole a glance over his shoulder, saw nobody; facing forward, he adjusted his grip on Holly's hand, picked up the pace with his automatic leading the way.

Reached the corner, peeked around. Clear. A step and—

Two of the three shooters appeared at the same time. Dane blasted a hole through the head of the closest man; the second shuffled back. Dane and the gunman fired at the same time. Holly screamed, her hand slipping from Dane's. Dane watched the gunman's body slam into one of the support poles of the overhang. And fired a second shot into his chest.

Dane looked back and saw Holly's body on the ground. She looked up at him with wide eyes.

"Come on!" Dane hauled her up. Gunshots on the other side of the building. Nina meeting the challenge of the last gunman. Dane half dragged Holly behind him as he ran for the Ford; off to the right, Nina charged across the blacktop with the same destination in mind.

Chapter Sixteen

Nina drove fast. Holly, who had been shoved into the back seat by Dane, shifted to the middle and leaned between the front seats.

"Some rescue," she said. "Tommy said you're this hot shot tough guy but all I've seen is an idiot whose girlfriend wears a dress and sandals to a gun fight."

"You're welcome," Nina said.

"You sound like one of those dumb Ruskies I met in Sri Lanka last year."

"You sound like one of those inbred rednecks."

"I'm not a redneck, I'm Mexican!"

"Same thing, honey."

"All right, stop! Both of you!" Dane shouted.

Nina tightened her grip on the wheel. She glanced once at Dane with her mouth a tight line.

Back at the hotel, Dane sat with a drink while Holly splashed in the shower. He made circles with the glass, swishing the bourbon on ice. Condensation from the glass left circular trails of water on the table. He stared at a spot on the carpet.

He had found Holly, yeah. But she and Nina were not going to get along. They were going to give him headaches.

He already had a headache going, thinking of all the missteps he'd made throughout the day. Somehow Thorne's bunch had picked up his trail, and he'd missed the gun crew at the motel.

Tunnel-vision. He was too focused on one thing and not seeing other things.

He had only vengeance on his mind. Not the first time. Not the last. He had to re-center and approach the problem coldly, same as before. He wasn't going to get another warning, and it wasn't only him who might get hurt or killed.

Nina huffed as she repacked clothes in a drawer, carefully folding each item before placing it inside.

"I can't believe that little mouse," she said, "pawing through my outfits and my undies with those cherry-picking hands of hers. At least my bras won't fit her. I get even a little there." She shut the drawer and turned to Dane. "Are you listening to me?"

"Something about your bras?"

"I thought so." Nina came over and picked up Dane's glass and took a sip. She sat on his lap and hooked an arm around his neck while he grabbed her waist. "What's on your mind?"

The shower stopped.

"We can't keep her here," Dane said. "We probably shouldn't stay here ourselves."

"That's not what you're thinking about, dummy."

"I could have gotten us all killed today," he said.

"But you didn't."

"That isn't the point. The point is I should have guessed Thorne and Skinner knew where she was the whole time. When I talked to Skinner on the phone, he knew it was me. My arrival wasn't a surprise. He said he had plenty of surprises and we just experienced one of them. They were coming right at us and I missed it."

"What about the goons in the Dodge?"

"A preemptive attempt to take us out and then get Holly. Which means, again, that we can't stay here."

Holly came out wearing one of Nina's dresses. The material sagged in front. She did a turn and said, "How do I look?"

"Too bad I don't have an extra jacket," Nina said. "Looks like it's a bit nippy out."

"Usted os un sucio puta."

"There's no reason to involve your mother in this," Nina said.

Holly's cheeks flared.

"Knock it off," Dane said. He gave Nina a nudge and she hopped off. He stood, took the glass from her and finished his drink. "We need to get moving."

Nina smiled. "Where?"

"I'll tell you when we get there. And then I need to do some serious thinking."

The bodies had been carried away, but the blood and property dam-age remained. The crime scene crew sorted through the worst of the mess while uniformed officers kept the parking lot blocked. Inspector Gino Vicini, his partner Jack Wade, and other investigators interviewed witnesses. After an hour of questioning the other guests, Vicini and Wade met up outside the motel office.

"Well?" Vicini said, turning his back to the parking lot. The flashing strobe lights atop the squad cars flashed his shadow off and on against the office wall.

"The manager says the occupant of number four was a

Hispanic woman who checked in alone." Wade read from his notes. "Name's Jane Garcia."

"Might as well be Jane Jones."

"Maybe you did better?"

"Got a witness says a man and two women took off in a compact car. The woman was wearing a blue dress and sandals."

"Let's go see Mr. Dane," Wade said.

Dane spotted Vicini and Wade as he entered the lobby. They stood near the front desk, Vicini in his jeans and flannel shirt while Wade, in his rumpled overcoat, looked like a reject from an old RKO movie. The pair followed him into the elevator. As the car started up, Dane said, "Pleasant evening?" Vicini glared. Wade hit the stop button.

Vicini spun Dane and pushed him against a wall. The wood paneling felt cold against his face. Vicini pressed against Dane's head, squishing his nose against the wall. Dane grunted but did not resist as the inspector patted him down.

Vicini stepped back. Dane turned around, straightened his clothes and rubbed his nose. Wade hit the go switch and the elevator resumed its ascension.

"Satisfied?"

"I didn't give you permission to shoot up the town," Vicini said.

The elevator stopped at Dane's floor and the three men stepped out into the quiet hallway. The cops looked up and down the hall. Dane waited with his hands outside his pockets.

Vicini said, "Where were you about an hour ago?"

"With my lady friend."

"I said where."

"Dinner."

"Where? I swear, Dane, if you jerk me around—"

"John's Grill. Dashiell Hammett used to eat there so I wanted to soak up the literary history."

Dane had noticed the restaurant while driving to the new hotel he'd taken the women to. He'd booked a two-room suite after Nina and Holly refused to stay in one room together.

Dane asked Vicini, "Why is my evening any business of yours?"

"Five dead gunmen at the Palace Motel."

"So?"

"I'm not a fool, Dane."

Dane glanced at Wade, who stood a little behind Vicini, moving his eyes between Dane's face and hands. He chewed gum mouth open. Dane smelled a hint of peppermint on his breath.

"Where's your lady friend now?" Vicini said.

"Browsing a dress shop somewhere. I don't have the patience for that, so I took a cab back here."

"You got an answer for everything," Vicini said.

"I never tell a lie," Dane said.

Vicini clenched his jaw.

"I better not regret our arrangement."

"I have a vested interest in making sure you don't. Can I go now?"

Vicini pressed the elevator button. The doors slid open. Dane watched the cops step inside. Wade kept his eyes on Dane as the door closed.

Dane grinned and entered his room, and quickly examined the area but nothing appeared to have been tampered with. Nobody hid in the closet, bathroom, or under the bed. As he placed his wallet and key card on the nightstand, he saw the red message light on the phone blinking.

He called the front desk.

"You had a visitor, sir. He said he couldn't reach you and left a note."

"What did he say?"

"'See you soon, love Dick and Joe.'"

"Thanks for letting me know."

Dane hung up and shook his head.

The visit and the note were nothing more than a psychological trick, but also a statement. They were two steps ahead and wanted him to know. Dane had taught them such tricks but, unlike the ambush, it wasn't a technique they had improved. If they had really wanted to ambush him, they'd have broken into the room and waited. Instead they wanted to mess with his mind.

Good luck with that.

He called Nina on his cell.

"You okay?" he said.

"No surprise guests if that's what you mean, but it would be nice if they turned up."

"Why?"

"This woman is driving me nuts. If I don't kill somebody else soon, I may kill her."

"I'll be there in a bit. Warm up the bed for me."

"No way, Mister Dane. I had a cot sent up for you. You are not sleeping in my bed tonight."

Dane laughed.

"I'm not laughing, darling," she said.

"You have to be nice to me. I have all of your outfits and undies, remember?"

"You're pushing it."

"Be there soon."

She huffed and hung up the phone. Dane quickly packed their belongings and departed.

Chapter Seventeen

"He wasn't there," said Dick "Skinner" McNab.

"Too bad," said Joe Thorne.

The two men sat in the living room of the house they had rented just outside the Dogpatch neighborhood, not far from the 280 freeway, and despite the distance from the freeway they could still hear the faint sounds of cars. Nobody asked too many questions about what went on in the neighborhood. It also wasn't their usual opulent quarters, but they didn't have the choice. Their employer wasn't exactly flush with cash.

McNab, dressed in a black suit, sat straight in his chair, legs crossed, hands on armrests. Thorne slumped a little, legs crossed at the ankles, hands dangling over the armrests, his wiry five-foot-five frame hardly concealed by baggy jeans and a black T-shirt.

Joe Thorne had always been the man in charge, even when they were kids. The pair had grown up together. Thorne was the son of a judge, and Skinner's old man was a state's attorney general. They had relied on, and received, protection from their respective daddies who did not want to answer for the rowdy youths as such accountability did not help reelection efforts.

But one could not keep their actions covered up forever. Thorne and McNab had been in their early twenties when they went out drinking one night. Both were so plastered by closing time that when the barman, a hulk of a guy, tried to escort them out, McNab, who would earn the nickname "Skinner" because of his skill with a blade, pulled such a weapon and stabbed the man ten times.

The incident made the news. The bartender almost died but pulled through. The parents of Thorne and McNab quietly arranged for their boys to get a minimum of punishment before being released to the streets, a move that a local talk show host exploited on his radio show. The public outcry barely rose above a whimper. With high unemployment, high gas prices, high food prices, and other matters of worry, the public was not sufficiently outraged about corrupt politicians to vote them out of office when the opportunity next came around.

Their fathers made the boys realize that they needed a change, that change was the military. They enlisted in the army and served in the same combat unit, where, one night in a bar, they met Steve Dane.

"He's stashed the woman elsewhere by now," Thorne said.

"And we're suddenly short-staffed."

"I'll handle that. Found a safecracker yet?"

"A contact introduced me to a police inspector who knows somebody we can use."

"A cop?"

"I'm meeting him in an hour."

"A cop."

"Right. Guy named Wade. Has a gambling debt.

Needs cash."

"How did you meet him?"

"My contact knows this cop from their poker club. The cop is willing to make a recommendation if we help him pay off the bill."

"Strange connection. This is going to get really complicated very soon."

"It's always complicated when Dane's around," McNab said.

"This hasn't been the easiest job we've ever done," Thorne said.

Inspector Second Grade Jack Wade sat in his car drumming fingers on the wheel as Rush played on the stereo. His overcoat lay on the passenger seat. He'd parked on the far end of the shopping center parking lot, the visor tipped down to block the glare from the tall lampposts lighting the lot. There were two open spaces on either side, and when another car approached and flashed its headlights, Wade shut off the music. His hands were shaking.

What he was doing tonight was not what a good cop was supposed to do. Wade felt, deep down, that he was a good cop, but he needed help because of his own poor choices. There was no denying that he had dug the hole for himself.

He'd been playing poker his whole life and playing well, with the usual ups and downs, but lately it had been all downs, and the money he had to pay back—borrowed to cover losses and stake the next win—was more than he could ever repay on his salary.

The only way to get clear of that anvil was to help a man named Skinner McNab find a safecracker. And tell him about Steve Dane. There should be a nice bonus in that.

The other car stopped facing the opposite direction. Wade lowered his window. Cool air drifted inside the car. Wade looked at Skinner McNab.

McNab said, "Find the man I need?"

"Yeah," Wade said, "but I think I have something else for you if you're willing to spend a little more money."

"Like what?"

"Like who's shooting up your guys. Don't play dumb, Skinner. I know the east coast shooters are yours. You all arrived about the same time. I know who's causing your problems, and I can help you find him."

"I already know who he is. What I need to know is where he is."

"I can tell you that."

"He's got a deal with your boss, doesn't he?"

"More like a short leash," Wade said.

"So?"

"He was at the Hyatt, but he's gone now."

"I'll give you another fifty grand when you deliver."

"I need eighty thousand."

"Sixty-five, no more."

Wade tapped the steering wheel. "Okay."

"Now the other thing."

Wade handed Skinner a folded sheet of paper. "John Pyle. Best on the street. Skinny guy with a limp. He'll crack your safe for you."

"Does he know you gave me his name?"

"Yup."

Skinner took the paper and handed Wade a shoebox in return. Wade pulled at the tape holding the lid, looked inside and saw money.

Wade put the shoebox on the passenger seat. He said, "See you soon," and drove off.

His hands still shook and his increased heartrate made it hard to breathe. He pulled over, jumped out of the car and stood leaning against the hood, taking long deep breaths. This wasn't going to hurt anybody. Right? Except maybe Steve Dane, and what did he matter? Wade kept breathing deep and running through the justifications in his head. None of them made him feel better.

Chapter Eighteen

Skinner called the safecracker while on the road and arranged a meeting. It was at a bar Skinner was familiar with and he told Pyle he'd be seated in a corner near the pool table.

Skinner sat with his back to the wall and watched the players around the tables, listening to the clack of balls slamming together followed by the thunk as they dropped into pockets. Rock music played over the digital jukebox but it wasn't too loud.

The door opened and a thin man with a limp walked in. Skinner watched him.

Pyle limped to the bar, ordered a beer, and approached Skinner's table. "You Skinner?"

"Sit."

Pyle set down the beer, and braced his hands on the table as he lowered onto the chair. "What's the job?"

"Safe in a house." Skinner handed the other man a stack of small photos. He watched Pyle sort through and examine each one.

"These were taken inside the house," Pyle said. "Nice."

"I can get by the security system, but I need you to

pop the box."

Pyle nodded. "When?"

"Tomorrow night."

"How much?"

"Fifteen thousand, half in advance."

Pyle smiled and stuck out his hand. "Deal."

Jack Wade carried the shoebox under his left arm as he entered the dimly lighted poker club. Low voices and the clicks of chips filled the room. Most of the tables were full. Wade spotted John Pyle at one, laughing as he collected a pot. Had Pyle met Skinner already?

As Wade watched Pyle play, another player at the table glared at him and Wade knew there would be a problem with that group. He waited at the counter. A bald Mexican sauntered over.

"'Lo, Jack."

Wade slid the shoebox across the counter, lifted the lid. "Fifteen."

"Still got a long way to go," the bald man said as he took the box.

"Another day or two and I'll be caught up."

"Okay." The bald man went away, and Wade turned to watch the tables. He wanted to play but couldn't get a seat until he'd paid off what he owed the club.

He looked back at the table John Pyle sat at. The safecracker slapped down his cards with an exclamation of victory, but his table mates weren't laughing. The man who had glared at him earlier pointed a finger across the table.

"I know a cheater when I see one," the man said.

Wade was glad Skinner had paid him in advance.

"We should keep the stuff for ourselves," Holly said. "Have you thought of that?"

Holly waited for Dane to respond but all he did was stare at the skyline.

The suite included a balcony. Dane, smoking one of his La Galera cigars, leaned against the rail with his back to Holly. Nina sat in a lounge chair to Dane's left sipping a glass of red wine.

Holly folded her arms. "Well?"

"The loot doesn't belong to you, Holly," Dane said.

"Oh, you're Moral Oral, now?"

Dane exhaled a cloud of smoke. "We recover the antiques, wipe out the trafficking network, then talk about splitting the reward for the loot, that's it."

"The reward is pennies compared to what we can get—"

"Stop it, Holly," Dane said. "There's more going on here than what to do with the money."

Holly glared at Dane.

Nina said, "What are we doing next?"

"I think of hitting the road," Holly said.

"Go if you want," Dane said. "We're going forward. This isn't about you, Holly. It's about Tom. It's about Sam Roca and good men who died trying to do the right thing. I had to leave Tom behind and it was one of the hardest things I've ever had to do. I'm not letting his killers get away with that."

Holly folded her arms and stared at Dane some more. He puffed his cigar and said nothing. Finally, she said, "Elliot Meyer is the man we need to see."

"Where does he live?"

"Marin County."

Dane nodded.

"Hear what happened at your poker club?" Vicini said.

Jack Wade sat at his desk, breaking off pieces of a large muffin, fallen crumbs mixing with the rest of the mess on his desktop. A large cup of coffee rested on top of a manila folder. Other papers and an open notebook with illegible pen scratches waited at his left elbow. Vicini sat down at his clean desk and popped the top on a can of Cherry Coke.

Jack Wade stopped a muffin piece halfway to his mouth. "What?"

"Somebody got shot. Somebody else accused the victim of cheating."

"Who got shot?"

"Guy named Pyle. Got a record. Safecracker."

"Really."

"Kirk and McHale found some pictures on him. Whoever owns the place is going to have a bad time very soon."

"Maybe Pyle was working alone."

Vicini shrugged. "Who knows? They haven't found anything in the pics to tell them where the house is, so we'll have to wait."

"No leads at all?"

"Nope."

"Maybe we should—"

"It's not our case, Jack. Not open, either. They got the shooter."

Jack put down the muffin piece.

"Not hungry?" Vicini said.

Wade glared at his partner.

Wade sat in his car, the windows rolled up. The car wasn't parked under any shade and the sun bled through the glass, baking the inside. Sweat covered Wade's brow, but not all of it was from the heat. Wade called Skinner. Skinner answered right away.

"You could not have found Dane this soon," Skinner said.

"No, something else," Wade said. He told Skinner about the Pyle shooting and the recovery of the pictures.

Skinner did not respond and let the silence linger a few moments. Then he said, "What about Dane?"

Wade also admitted that he had no leads on Dane. Skinner hung up.

Wade looked at his phone a moment, stowed it, and exited the car. The outside air cooled him a bit. He wiped his forehead with the palm of his hand, brushed his hand on his trousers, and crossed the lot back to the headquarters building. He turned his head from side to side as he walked. There were other people around, but nobody noticed him.

Chapter Nineteen

Dane and Nina and Holly had split up to cover the Meyer family and
see what they did with themselves. Dane stayed with Elliott, the father, following the man to his office where he
spent a few hours, then trailing him to a country club where
he played eighteen holes with two other men. Nina, following the kids, noted that Meyer and his wife must have
had them when they were older—both Elliott and his wife
Julie were in their early fifties while the oldest child, son
Jeff, was only fourteen; daughter Erika was ten.

Dane caught up with Elliott after the golf game. Meyer
bid farewell to his partners, loaded the clubs into the trunk,
and paused to clip and light a cigar. As he took the first few
puffs, he leaned against the trunk of his car and surveyed
the grounds. Dane wandered over with his own cigar out
and said, "Got a light?"

Meyer nodded and handed Dane a box of matches.
Dane fired up his La Galera and shared a few words with
Meyer on the merits of their tobacco selections and the
weather and the sand trap before the fifteenth hole. Meyer
had clear and confident eyes that did not look at Dane's

very often. Instead, he looked around as he spoke, as if
Dane wasn't really there.

Dane said, "We have a mutual friend."

"Really?"

"Sam Roca."

"You know Sam? From where?"

"You don't understand," Dane said, and told him what
was going on.

"You've been watching me?"

"So have they."

"Get out of here."

"Your family is at risk, Meyer. Give me your map piece
and I'll steer the threat away."

"I said beat it."

Dane flicked back his jacket to expose the holstered
Detonics .45. "I'm not fooling around. Neither are they."

"I don't need any help," Meyer said, "and your gun
doesn't scare me." Meyer climbed into his car and drove
away.

Dane watched the car leave the parking lot. He puffed
on his cigar. If that's how Meyer wanted to play, he
could turn up the heat, or wait until Thorne and Skinner
made their move.

The Meyer home had been built not far from the Richmond-San
Rafael Bridge, with a view of the bay and the county ma-
rina. A wrought-iron fence stretched around the property.
A two-lane road led past the house. Dane had parked a few
miles away and hiked through a field to a rise where he
dropped prone. He dug his elbows into the soft dirt. The
road, which curved around the home, lay between Dane
and the house. The bay water splashed up on the coast off
to his left. Dane had taken his Detonics .45, which had a

barrel extension so it could take a silencer, and the gun, fitted with such a suppressor, under his left arm. Just in case.

Dane scanned the property through a pair of binoculars. Lights on in front and inside, the large swimming pool lit up in back. The evening was warm enough for a dip, Dane thought. He sweated under his long coat.

He angled the binoculars to examine the slope of dirt before the fence and the shadows didn't look right. Was somebody hiding there?

A motor hummed off to the left. Dane turned that way. A van. It didn't continue around the curve but instead pulled to the shoulder and stopped. Dane zoomed in. The van had halted near a telephone pole and a man, dressed in black similar to Dane, leapt out and climbed the pole to the junction box. Dane couldn't see the man's movements since he blended into the night sky, but he knew what the man was doing.

Dane swung back to the fence. The shadows came to life—men with slung weapons. They scaled the fence. Gunfire crackled from elsewhere on the property. Dane watched the fence climbers crash through the back-patio doors.

Dane left the binoculars behind and bolted toward the van, his boots thumping on the asphalt. Another crackle of gunfire. Dane neared the van, drawing the silenced .45. As the man who climbed the pole descended and touched down, Dane fired twice. The man fell back. Dane opened the van, the other occupant spinning to look at him. Dane shot him in the head. The man fell out of his chair. In front of the dead man was a radio set. Dane went to the first man and yanked a walkie-talkie and earpiece from his kit.

He fitted the earpiece and listened.

"Side yard secure."

"Back secure."

Dane searched the van. He found no other weapons. He would have to mount a counterassault alone, armed only with a pistol, against an unknown number of opponents.

Just another night out.

Earlier, when Dick "Skinner" McNab had learned of John Pyle's death, he told Thorne. They agreed there wasn't time to find another box breaker. Thorne told Skinner he would have to do the job himself.

"How?" Skinner had said.

"Stick a gun in Meyer's face and make him open the safe."

"I guess I'll need some men."

Skinner waited with three other gunners on the slope beside the wrought-iron fence of the Meyer home. When they jumped the fence and broke through the patio doors, Skinner had the lead.

The gunman powered into the living room. The family, who had been focused on the wide screen television, screamed and jumped from the couch. Julie Meyer grabbed for Jeff and Erika; Elliott Meyer stepped in front of them. He made eye contact with Skinner and started moving his mouth, but Skinner did not bother to make sense of the words. He aimed at the exposed leg of the son and fired once. The bullet punched through a spot above the boy's knee and he screamed, fell. His mother dropped beside him.

Skinner turned the smoking muzzle of his machine pistol at Meyer; the father put up both hands, palms forward.

"Open your safe."

Meyer, hands raised, started up the spiral staircase with Skinner right behind him. They went down a hallway to an office where Meyer lifted a painting off the wall, revealing the safe. He started twisting the dial with a shaking hand but had to stop and start again. As he moved through the combination sequence a second time, automatic weapons fire exploded below. Meyer spun around and struck Skinner with a fist, but Skinner only grunted and smashed the barrel of the machine pistol across Meyer's head. The man dropped unconscious. Skinner ran back down the hallway. As he reached the staircase, he heard a man's voice: "Stay down!"

Chapter Twenty

Dane knelt by the front of the van, pressing the earpiece to his left ear. He spotted the commandos every time one moved – light from the streetlamp splashed enough of a glow to show their outlines.

Bad news: He only had a pistol.

Good news: He looked just like them.

Dane moved from the van bent at the waist, holding the .45 close to his body. As he reached the driveway gate, one commando turned to look at him. A second stood a few feet away.

"You aren't supposed to leave the van."

Dane straightened with the .45 and shot the commando in the head. The second gunman started to shoulder his submachine gun; Dane swung that way and fired twice. Second man down.

How many more?

Dane stowed the .45 and snatched the first gunner's SMG and spare clips. It was a familiar weapon, a Heckler & Koch MP7. Dane jammed the stock into his right shoulder and started prowling, staying close to the edge of the fence.

He stopped after a few feet. A black lump with legs lay on the grass. Dane stepped closer. A Border Collie. Shot through the head. Dane mashed his teeth and stepped over the dead animal.

Chatter in his ear: "Side yard clear."

Dane dropped to one knee. He saw the two other gunners ahead, near the house. He wondered which one had shot the dog.

"Front? Are you there, front? Jimmy, come in."

Another voice, from inside the house. "Is there a problem?" Dane heard the Meyer family in the background.

"Checking."

Dane felt for the HK's safety. It was off. The gunman approached, one still calling on the radio. When they neared, Dane rose. The gunners paused a second too long. Dane burned through the magazine, the crackle of gunfire filling the night. He was on the move across the driveway and reloading before the bodies landed on the ground.

Another gunner was two feet out the front door when Dane gained the porch. Dane fired first, the gunner tumbling down the steps. Dane jumped over the body, pushing through the door. He blasted the next closest commando in the chest. As the man fell, Dane shouted, "Stay down," and acquired the next target. He fired, then shifted to the last gunner; flame flashed from the last commando's weapon. A slug tugged at Dane's ear, parted his hair. Dane stitched the commando belly to neck.

Boots pounded the stairs. Steve Dane sprang to his feet, sweeping the staircase with the HK's muzzle. Dick McNab came down those steps and raised his weapon; Dane dived to the right, landing near a dining table, as Skinner's rounds tore up the walls. Dane fired without aiming, missed, and the HK clicked empty. Skinner let out a yell, dropping his empty machine pistol and drawing a knife. He surged forward and jumped, sailing over the table. Dane swung the HK, deflecting the knife as Skinner landed. Skinner rolled a few feet. Dane took out the .45, firing, the rounds cutting through the carpet. Skinner, on his feet, lunged for the open door. Dane fired again and hit the frame. Skinner slipped into the night. Dane ran after him. Skinner didn't stop to grab a weapon, and Dane fired again and again as Skinner sprinted for the street.

Dane holstered his empty pistol and grabbed another HK off a dead gunner. He sprinted across the front yard, breathing hard, lungs burning, sweat dripping down his face. He reached the gate, looked up and down the street. No sign of Skinner. He could have gone any direction. Dane moved his head left and right, hoping for a sign, but nothing anywhere betrayed Skinner's position.

And, now, sirens in the distance. Always sirens, Dane thought. He wiped his forehead and ran for the car. His business with Elliott Meyer would have to wait.

"Most of the men we hired are dead, Skinner," Thorne said from the couch, on the only cushion that wasn't stained or torn. Lights lit the room; the drapes were closed.

Skinner paced the floor.

"Moping won't get us anywhere. "Dane is still as good as ever," Thorne said. "But we're not dragging the bag either. We still have a way."

"The daughter," Skinner said.

Dane caught up with Meyer the next afternoon.

The incident at his home made the news, though neither the cops nor the family said much. The local media wasn't easily put off, though, but none of that concerned Dane.

Dane first tried Meyer's office, but he'd called in sick. Dane staked out the hospital where Meyer's son Jeff had been taken. He wandered around most of the day, and eventually spotted Meyer in the parking lot.

Meyer did not walk confidently. He moved with slumped shoulders, hands shaking as he fumbled for his keys. Dane stepped up beside the other man. "Got a light?" he said.

Meyer stiffened and sucked air. "You—"

"Should have listened to me at the golf course."

Meyer remained rigid. "With what happened to Sam—"

"I'm here to help. Get in."

Meyer unlocked the doors. Dane dropped into the passenger seat before Meyer had his door closed. Outside noise didn't leak through. The soft leather seat felt like a couch; Dane shifted to better see Meyer. He tucked the .45 back under his coat.

Meyer, head down a little, stared at the emblem on the steering wheel.

"What do you want me to do?"

"I need your piece of the map," Dane said. "Once I have that I'll lead them away."

"But I know too much. They'll still want to kill me and my family. The smugglers won't be stopped."

"Then you know what you have to do. Make yourself scarce. Once I solve the problem it'll be safe for you to come back."

Meyer let out a breath. He stared at his lap for a while. "I guess we can go back to the house and I'll get my part of the map," he finally said.

"Buckle up," Dane said.

Meyer's cell phone rang. He answered. As he listened the color drained from his face.

Chapter Twenty-One

Dane returned to his car after giving Meyer instructions to wait while he made the exchange arrangements. He wasn't going to risk another gun battle with an innocent now in the crossfire.

He pressed redial on the captured cell phone.

Skinner picked up the other end. "I wondered how long it would take you to call," he said.

"What are you thinking, Skinner? Kidnapping a teenage girl is not professional."

"You done?"

"I'll bring you the map pieces. Tonight. You bring the girl, unharmed."

"There's an abandoned drive-in theater on Monterey Road in San Jose," Skinner said. "Three AM."

"You'll be under a gun the whole time," Dane said. "No tricks."

"We'll be there by proxy."

"You mean you still have men left?"

"You're funny. And Dane?"

"Hmmm."

"The map pieces better be the real ones."

"See you soon, Skinner."

"One way or another. Can't wait."

Nina lay prone beside Dane on the gravel-and-tar topped roof of the empty drive-in movie theater. If it had been a happening place during its day one could not prove it now. The screens were peeling at the edges and torn in sections, and the metal speaker posts standing in neat rows throughout the parking lot now rusted away.

With every gust of wind, the roof creaked, but Dane and Nina weren't worried about the boarded-up structure collapsing. If something were to go wrong tonight, the roof caving in would not be that something.

Dane, laying on a mat to protect his knees and elbows from the tar-and-gravel roof, checked his watch. Almost time. His Detonics Scoremaster lay on the mat in front of him but he wished for a good rifle. A .45 wasn't built for long range.

Nina, on a duplicate mat, watched the entrance to the drive-in through binoculars.

Presently a black car pulled into the drive-in. The vehicle made a circuit of the empty lot, the tires crunching debris on the blacktop, then settled with the front facing the exit. Two minutes later, Meyer's car pulled in and stopped a few feet from the first car's front end. Doors opened on both vehicles. Meyer stood by the driver's side of his car. Two men who were not Joe Thorne or Skinner McNab exited the other car.

The men exchanged words. Meyer held up the envelope containing the map pieces; one of Thorne's men bent down, leaned into his car long enough to haul out a tied and gagged Erika Meyer. The man gave her a push and she shuffled toward her father's car. Meyer put the envelope on the hood, grabbed his daughter, and helped her into his car. Thorne's goon came over and took the envelope. Meyer just looked at him. The goon pivoted and went back to his car.

Thorne's men checked the envelope, hopped back in the car, and drove away. Meyer made a quick U-turn and screeched his tires speeding off.

Dane let out a breath.

"We could have taken them once the girl was safe," Nina said.

"I'm not playing games with the girl's life."

"You're such a boy scout," she said.

"You know me better than that, honey," Dane said. "I was never a boy scout."

The next morning Dane left the hotel early to tie up a few loose ends.

He visited Meyer first at the hotel where the man's family was staying. They talked in the bar.

"You're lucky," Dane told him. "You still need to disappear."

"What about Thorne?"

"He's moved on by now."

"Vegas or Arizona?"

"Does it matter?"

When Dane finished with Meyer, he visited police headquarters and found Inspectors Vicini and Wade. Vicini suggested they move to the parking lot for their chat, and the cops led Dane to a covered sitting area on the side of the building. The spot was bookended by grass and flowers. A shade of brown attacked the grass and the flowers looked anorexic.

Vicini said, "You've been hard to find the last few days.

Should I even ask?"

"All you need to know," Dane said, "is that I'm leaving town."

"The only reason for that is—"

"Right."

"God help whoever you run into next," Vicini said. "I enjoyed that cigar, by the way."

"Good."

"The mess we've had to clean up—"

"I totally upset the natural order, didn't I?"

"You're good at it."

Wade jumped in. "The bad guys are dead, Gino. No real people got hurt. Let's call it a day on this."

Vicini smiled. "In the beginning Wade wanted to lock you up."

"Smart man," Dane said. "I'll send you that case of smokes. Inspector Wade looks like a whiskey man."

"Gentleman Jack."

"Done. Well. I guess I'll take my leave."

Dane shook hands with the detectives. Vicini and Wade went back inside and Dane returned to his car.

Halfway down the hall, Wade told Vicini he wanted to get something out of his car. "Be right back," he said.

Wade ran to his car as Dane turned left out of the driveway. Wade weaved between cars to catch up.

His last conversation with Skinner McNab, only two hours earlier, ran through his head.

"We're pulling out but our deal still stands if you find Dane, and keep him from following us."

"I'll do what I can," Wade had said, though at the time he had no clue how to accomplish the mission. He wished he'd never made the offer in the first place.

But now, he had his chance.

Wade pulled up alongside Dane's car, tooted the horn. Dane looked over. Wade gestured towards a park on the corner. Dane steered that way. Wade followed. They parked curbside. Dane climbed out. Wade exited his car. Wade examined the other man. Dane stood there in his fancy black clothes, his shoulders straight, confident and sure of himself, his head tilted a little as he waited for Wade to speak. Wade felt a flush crawl up his neck. Dane was everything he wasn't yet wanted so much to be. He said, "I'm sorry, there's one more thing."

"What?"

Wade took out his gun. "Against the car."

"Hey—"

"None of your lip. Move!"

Dane put his hands on the roof of the hot car, legs spread; Wade patted him down and stepped back.

"Get over there by those trees."

"This is a park."

"There isn't anybody around. Go."

Dane and Wade crossed the dry grass, some of it rust-colored with patches of dirt, to a pair of trees standing beside one another. Their shade blocked the sun.

"Stop. Turn around."

Dane faced Wade. "Now what?"

"Nothing personal, Dane, but Skinner has money and I need some of it."

"Skinner's gone."

"He'll still pay me if I keep you from finding him."

"What do you need the money for?"

"None of your business."

"Come on, one scoundrel to another."

"No."

"Fine. What did Skinner offer?"

"You gonna try and double it?"

"Triple. If you let me go."

"But Skinner—"

"There won't be any more Skinner once I find him. If you need this money so bad, you surely don't care where it comes from."

Wade swallowed.

"How much?"

"Sixty-five thou."

"Close to two hundred thousand, no problem."

"You have it now?"

"We can go to where it is," Dane said. "It has to be wired from overseas."

"All right," Wade said.

"Chuck that rosco."

Wade pushed back the flap of his coat. As he slipped the automatic back into his holster, Dane punched him. Wade fell to the side, stunned. Dane grabbed Wade's wrist, twisted the arm away, and kneed him in the groin. As the inspector cried out Dane punched him again. Wade collapsed.

Dane took Wade's cell phone and went back to his car. He drove away while searching the call history for Vicini's number.

"Where are you, Jack?"

"It's Dane. Go to St. Mary's Park. Wade's unconscious by some trees. When he wakes up ask him why he tried to kill me."

"Wait, what?"

Dane tossed the phone out the window.

Chapter Twenty-Two

When Dane returned to his suite, he told Nina what had happened with Wade.

She said, "I'm sorry I missed all the fun. We're all packed."

"Then let's go to Arizona," he said.

"I bet it's going to be hot."

"Don't worry," Dane said. "It's a dry heat."

Casa Grande, Arizona

"At least it's warmer than San Francisco," Nina said. "Where else can it be 90-degrees in February?"

Dane said, "Uh-huh."

They stood on the balcony of their hotel room, looking out across rooftops to a pair of rugged mountains. The city sat under a clear blue sky. Dane was already starting to sweat under his long-sleeved shirt, so he turned back the cuffs.

"Will it be too warm to smoke your cigars?" Nina said.

Dane only smiled and went back into the room. He placed a suitcase on the bed and began taking out clothes and other items. He placed everything on the bed.

Nina leaned against the dresser. Arms folded, she said, "What's bothering you now?"

"I don't like getting beaten."

"We haven't lost anything yet," she said.

Dane sat on the bed. "It's more than that. I paid for college by playing poker at a small casino," he said. "One night I missed a pot because I folded too early. I knew better, but I quit anyway, and it made me so upset that I blew the rest of what money I had chasing the next win."

"And the lesson is?"

"It happens. Thorne grabbing Meyer's daughter. I should have known, but it happened. We got through it. But during our ride here I've been so pissed off I'm afraid I might screw up something else."

"Aren't you glad I'm here to keep you on track?"

He went over to her, pulling her close. She felt warm and her hair smelled like strawberries.

"I guess that's the difference between then and now," he said. "Where were you the first time I needed you?"

"You didn't deserve me then."

He leaned in for a kiss as she tilted her head and then somebody knocked on the door.

Nina pulled him against her. "Ignore it."

Dane broke away. "It's Holly."

"Don't."

He answered the door and Holly Mendoza stepped inside. Nina folded her arms.

Dane said: "Well?"

Holly nodded. "I found him."

Holly drove with the AC full blast. It was almost enough to cool them down. She followed Cottonwood Lane, staying in the right lane, and Dane watched a whole lot of nothing flash by. Telephone poles, palm trees, assorted homes, but mostly empty desert and rocks. A few lots displayed construction activity. Casa Grande was growing, just not very fast. Dane adjusted the AC vent to blow on his sweaty neck.

"Grimmer owns a paper company now. It's another mile or two down the road."

The ride was already wearing on him. Or maybe this leg of the chase was making him anxious.

Holly turned into an office park, passing Grimmer & Son Paper and stopping the car across from the neighboring building. She parked in reverse so they could watch the front door.

The front door opened and a man, tall and skinny with thick black hair, locked up and dropped behind the wheel of a silver Lexus. He started the car.

"That's him," Holly said. She followed Grimmer onto the street.

But then they made a left turn and started deeper into downtown. Bars. Pawn shops. A strip-club. Grimmer stopped at none of those and kept driving.

"I thought Nina would have come with us."

"Don't worry about her."

"I'm sorry we don't get along."

"You two didn't exactly start on the right foot," he said. "Give her time."

They followed Grimmer past shops and restaurants. An elementary school. Grimmer turned right. He pulled into a church parking lot. St. Gertrude the Beloved. Holly cruised by. Dane watched Grimmer get out and cross the lot to the front entrance.

Holly parked down the street at the curb where a neighborhood of single-level homes began.

Dane unbuckled his seatbelt.

"You're going in?"

"Go back to the hotel," Dane said. "I'll get a cab back."

"Why?"

"I want to be alone when I talk to him."

"But if Thorne—"

"I'll be fine."

"Are you armed?"

"No." He opened the door as Holly dug her 9mm auto-loader out of her purse.

"Here," she said.

"I'm not bringing a gun into a church." Dane shut the door.

He went up the brick steps and pulled open the heavy oak door. It shut on its own power and sealed him inside.

He stepped through the entryway, skipping the holy water. Nobody sat in the pews and the well-lit altar, with the huge figure of Christ on the cross, occupied the traditional place in front. Off to the left a man and woman exited the candle loft, the woman carrying a sleeping baby. Dane stepped out of the entryway as the couple left. He peeked inside the loft but saw only lit candles, no Martin Grimmer.

Dane walked up the aisle and took a seat on the second row. Muffled voices drifted his way. The confession booths were off to the left. Dane crossed his legs and prepared for a wait. He glanced at the hanging Christ. His mother had been the religious one in the family. She had taken Dane and his brother to Mass every chance she could, usually when their father was on deployment somewhere. She had always told him, "God has plans for you," but as he sat in a church unfamiliar yet the same as the one he'd visited during his youth, he thought about his statement to Vicini about leaving a bona fide legacy. Is this what his mother had in mind?

It was the kind of question he didn't like to think about. He decided it was better to let his life play out and decide in his final moments.

A priest left one of the confessionals. Dane acknowledged the man with a nod. The man smiled and exited the sanctuary via a side door.

Dane watched the other booths but nobody else emerged for ten minutes. That's when Martin Grimmer finally showed himself. He zipped up his coat and started up the aisle.

"Mr. Grimmer."

The other man stopped and looked at Dane. He stood with stooped shoulders and a long face.

"Maybe you should confess to somebody else," Dane said.

"Who are you?"

"Steve Dane. I think you know why I'm here."

"What do you want?"

Dane scooted over. "Sit down."

"No."

"I want your map piece, Martin."

Grimmer started to walk away, stopped, turned back. "Maybe we should talk." He sat beside Dane and let out a breath.

"You're lucky I found you first," Dane said. He told Grimmer about the events in San Francisco.

"Meyer left me a message," Grimmer said, "but I didn't call him back."

"You won't be out of danger even if you give me the piece," Dane said.

"I need to atone somehow," Grimmer said. "There

didn't seem to be anything wrong at the time."

"What do you mean?"

"What started as something noble has deteriorated into violence and death," Grimmer said. "That wasn't supposed to happen."

Dane could have argued that Grimmer was being naive, but there was no reason to aggravate the man.

Grimmer pressed his lips together.

Dane pressed on. "My motives are personal," he said. "I'm not going to deny that."

"I wouldn't expect you to."

"Give me your piece of the map and I can take some of the pressure off."

"That treats the symptoms but doesn't solve the problem."

"We can go back to your place and get the piece, can't we?"

"What kind of man are you, Mr. Dane?"

Dane frowned.

"Are you a good man or a bad man?"

"I'm not sure—"

"Tell me."

Dane considered his answer.

"I'm not perfect."

Grimmer sniffed and went silent for a while. Dane wondered if his answer was good enough.

"If I give you my piece, I need to know something."

"What?"

"Your secret. Tell me something you hide."

Dane unbuttoned the cuff of his right sleeve, rolled the sleeve up a little, and showed Grimmer the puckered, fire-damaged skin on his arm.

"How did you get that?"

"Helicopter crash," Dane said.

"Why do you keep it hidden?"

Dane blinked a few times.

"Answer me," Grimmer said.

"Part of me is afraid how people will react, but the guy who was with me on the helicopter got burned worse than me, and he doesn't cover up. I think the truth is that I don't like seeing a reminder that I'm not invincible."

"We're all invincible when we're young," Grimmer said.

"Neither of us is young anymore," Dane said.

"I think you've passed the test. We can go back to my house and I'll give you my part of the map."

"Okay."

They left the church. As they approached Grimmer's car, another vehicle entered the lot. The new arrival stopped short. Dane and the driver locked eyes.

Skinner.

Dane shoved Grimmer toward his car. "Get out of here."

Grimmer scrambled for his vehicle.

Dane approached Skinner's car and stood between it and Grimmer. As Grimmer's car screeched onto the street, Skinner stepped out of his.

"If I know you, Dane, you aren't carrying a gun."

Dane smiled.

Chapter Twenty-Three

Skinner slammed his door. "But I don't need a gun to deal with you."

Skinner took out his knife and charged. Sunlight flashed off the blade as Skinner swung at Dane's face. Dane ducked under the blade and punched Skinner just above the stomach. Skinner only staggered back, sucking air. Dane hit enough hard muscle to know the blow hadn't delivered the damage he'd intended.

Dane faked a lunge, stopping short, as he and Skinner circled each other. Skinner tried to close the gap by slashing his blade at Dane's face, but the reach wasn't far enough.

The punch might not have taken Skinner out, but his short breaths and watery eyes showed Dane he hadn't been far off.

"Hurt, didn't it?" Dane said.

"Not enough."

Skinner lunged again and his arcing knife tore open Dane's shirt. As the blade dragged through the silk weave Dane grasped Skinner's wrist, twisting, Skinner's body following the forced movement and colliding with Dane.

Dane turned and pulled Skinner over his back in a classic judo move. The knife clattered on the ground behind Dane as Skinner landed on the pavement in front of him.

Dane drew his right foot back to kick; Skinner grabbed Dane's left ankle and pulled him off balance. Dane fell sideways and struck the fender of Skinner's car. Stunned and winded, Dane rolled away from the car, scrambled to hands and knees, and looked for the knife. It lay only a foot away.

Dane dived for the blade as Skinner gained his feet. Dane started to rise. Skinner kicked. The blow snapped back Dane's right hand—the one holding the knife—and the knife went flying. Dane met Skinner's next lunge and the two slammed together, Skinner going for Dane's neck. Dane turned and blocked Skinner's momentum with his left leg. They rotated as they fell, Dane landing on top, striking Skinner with his left elbow. He couldn't make a fist with his right hand.

Skinner grabbed one of Dane's ears, yanked; Dane screamed, rolled to his right to break the hold.

Both men didn't move for a moment, each one winded, hurt, and slowing down. Skinner moved first, crawling toward his knife. Dane watched him, unable to counteract. When Skinner picked up the knife and started back toward Dane, Dane removed both of his shoes and picked up one in his left hand.

Skinner laughed and closed in. Dane blocked Skinner's swings with the shoe, trying for a strike on the other man's face or wrist. Both continued the fight, each unsteady—

And then beefy hands and equally large men in police uniforms pulled them apart. When Dane was face first on the ground, handcuffs tightening his arms behind his back, he saw the patrol cars parked curbside. The cops were talking but Dane had no comprehension of their words. His right hand and wrist flared, sending hot bolts of pain through his body.

The cops put them in separate patrol cars. Dane slumped in the back, which smelled of body odor and vomit, and glanced back at the church as he was driven away.

The priest stood on the steps watching them go.

"Tell me your name," the dark-haired cop with the thick arms said. He spoke as if his vocal cords were a woodchipper and the words produced were bits of ground-up branches.

Dane sat in the chair beside the officer's desk and kept his own mouth shut.

He'd entered the country under his own name. Of all the stupid decisions he'd ever made...

"Your name."

Nina would give him ten kinds of hell for this.

"Hey! Want me to break your other hand? What's your name?"

His right hand wasn't broken; maybe it was sprained. Whichever, it still hurt, though he was getting some feeling back in his fingers and he could move them again.

Dane said, "Stephen Richard Dane."

The cop typed on his computer. The side of the monitor facing Dane displayed a pattern of grime, the source of which was anyone's guess.

"Address."

"Austria."

"Where?"

"Austria. Not Australia. Big difference."

"Maybe you don't know what you're looking at, smart mouth. We have you and your pal on assault with a deadly weapon and disturbing the peace. The jail has plenty of room and we get a little bored sometimes so don't think we'll just let you walk out of here."

"I'm an American citizen, but I live in Austria." Dane provided his street address.

"You're here on a visit?"

"Vacation."

"Who's the other guy?"

"Apparently a Protestant."

The cop pounded once on the desk. The computer jumped an inch. The cop pointed a fat finger at Dane. "I'm not telling you again. Behave." He straightened the monitor. "You got ID or a passport?"

"Not on me."

"Gonna be a long night, smart mouth."

A female officer with a rear end bigger than her head fingerprinted Dane and placed him in the holding cell. The cell wasn't much larger than a pair of closets glued together with a cot on both sides and a toilet in between.

Skinner McNab lay on one of the cots. Dane stretched out on the other. "This is living."

The lady cop shut the cell and locked it.

Skinner laughed. "Of all the places to end up."

"If you had half a brain we wouldn't be here."

"If you had let me cut you—"

"Don't make me come over there, Skinner."

Skinner laughed. "You realize we have a bigger problem?"

"I was thinking the same thing."

"We aren't going to be very popular with our friends."

Dane stretched out on the cot with his hands at his sides.

"You can't be surprised, you know, about this," Skinner said. "We're all from the same litter. We're all a bunch of savages. Our paths were bound to cross again."

"I'm not a savage."

"We don't belong in polite society," Skinner said. "You make a good effort at being a fancy pants and a do-gooder but if there weren't any money in it, you'd be doing the same thing we do."

"That's where you're wrong. I have all the money I need. Anything I pick up now is gravy."

"Ooooh, somebody won the lottery. Somebody's a hot shot."

"Somebody sounds jealous."

Skinner let out a low chuckle. "I don't have to convince you. Deep down you already know."

"There's one way I'm going to prove you wrong, Skinner."

"How's that?"

"I'm going to put a bullet in your head for what you did to Tom."

"Well," Skinner said, "we all have a dream."

Chapter Twenty-Four

Skinner snored while Dane lay awake.

The chat reminded him of another recent encounter with a former ally, one that hadn't ended well, despite Dane's efforts to avoid a fight. Why were so many of his ex-employees going bad? Maybe they were always bad eggs just looking for opportunity. It was the common nature of man. Leave him to his own devices and he'll serve only his own interest.

But, really, wasn't he doing the same thing? How did that make him the same as Skinner? It didn't. They might have similarities, but they were far apart. It all depended on the choices a man made, or the choices Fate made for him. Dane never could have followed the same path as Skinner, not the way he was raised. Maybe that was the true difference. Fate had provided an upbringing that taught Dane to put others first. Skinner had not been so fortunate.

Eventually he dozed off thinking about the bail hearing set for the morning. Only a few hours away.

The courtroom at least had some modern appointments like padded benches. The AC blew cold. Dane and Skinner, each with a court-appointed lawyer, pled not guilty and the judge set bail with orders for neither to leave town.

A stone-faced Nina led Dane down the court steps to the car. Thorne and Skinner went in a separate direction. Dane watched them go to their car.

"Steve?"

Nina's voice broke the spell. Dane opened the door and dropped onto the seat. Nina drove off.

"You're a jailbird," she said. "A hardened ex-con. Did you have to resort to man-sex to stay alive?"

"Stop it, honey."

"I should be pissed, right?"

"Maybe. But you're crazy in love with me and it was just bad luck."

"It'll be worse luck if the cops interfere."

"We'll be fine. The hard part is done. We'll go see Grimmer and wrap this up."

"And skip bail?"

Dane laughed. "Let them catch me. Interpol would love to list me as a fugitive among the rest of my so-called crimes."

Dane knocked. Martin Grimmer answered the door with a gun in his hand.

"Whoa," Dane said. "Remember me?"

Grimmer put the gun behind his back. "Mr. Dane. I'm sorry. Ever since—"

"I know. Cops arrested me and Skinner. We both made bail. I got here first."

"Come in."

Grimmer led Dane through the modestly furnished home

to the kitchen. Dane accepted a beer. They sat at a table beside a window that overlooked the large backyard garden.

"I was hoping you'd show," Grimmer said. "I'm not sure what to do."

"Once they know I have your map piece, they won't care about you."

"Because you're going to shoot me."

"If I wanted to shoot you, I wouldn't be talking."

"And you aren't frightened of my gun."

"Oh, that. Seen one, seen 'em all."

"Well," Grimmer said, "here." He pulled the envelope from the back pocket of his jeans and tossed it on the table.

Dane picked up the envelope but did not open it. The drawn look on Grimmer's face told him that he did not need to open it.

"You better get going. We don't have anything else to talk about."

"You can't stay here and fight Thorne and Skinner. You won't win."

Grimmer shook his head. "Leave, Mr. Dane. This is my fight. If they win, I know you'll avenge me. And the others."

Grimmer didn't wear the face of a man who could be reached anyway. He had made his decision.

"You can't win on your own," Dane said. "I'll stay."

"Leave," Grimmer said. "Right now."

Dane drove away with his hands tight on the wheel. He had the map piece but felt no sense of victory. Something bad was going to happen in the Grimmer house. He was going to try and shoot either Skinner or Thorne or whoever showed up, but there was no way for him to win such a fight. He wanted to go back and stand with the man, but Grimmer had insisted on standing alone. Dane was torn between turning around anyway because the hell with it, or staying on course.

What Skinner said in jail was getting under his skin. He had something to prove to both of them and maybe himself, too. He wanted to get back to Nina and Holly and move on to the next point in the journey and finish proving the point.

Dane took a deep breath. He had needed to turn around. He needed to keep driving. He had never been one to second guess any choice he made; now, he had no answers. Not for the past, or the present, and certainly not the future.

And when two police cars screamed past going the way he'd come he knew it was too late to change his mind.

Skinner stopped at the front door. The porch was dark. He lifted a hand to knock but when he did, the door inched open. The hinges squeaked. He stepped into the dark house and flicked a light switch on the right. He'd been there before.

Grimmer sat on the couch holding the revolver in his lap.

"Wanna holster that thing?" Skinner said.

"Dane has my envelope," Grimmer said.

"How about that."

Grimmer raised the gun. "I'm not fooling around. Get out."

Skinner stepped forward Grimmer fired one shot.

The slug hit the wall and shards pelted Skinner's face. He bent at the knees and started to draw his own pistol but Grimmer, on his feet now, raised the gun and fired again. The shot split the air above Skinner's head. Skinner fired twice into Grimmer's chest. The older man stood a moment longer, the light fading from his eyes, and his body collapsed onto the couch. Skinner regarded the dead man with wide eyes, then split. Things were getting complicated, indeed. Things always became complicated when Steve Dane was around.

Last Vegas, Nevada

The Excelsior Hotel was the new kid on the Vegas Strip, having been built five years before, and it had quickly gained a reputation as one of the nicest hotel/casinos in the city. That wasn't saying much, as many also claimed the title, but business had been good since opening day. Dane, Nina, and Holly witnessed the action as they entered the high-ceilinged lobby. The ground-level casino (there were three levels, accessible either by elevator or stairway) sat adjacent to the lobby. They had to walk by the rows of one-armed bandits in order to reach the elevators. A handful of guests, bags at their feet, fed coins into the slots for a few quick spins before venturing upward.

Dane was not a fan of Vegas. Too much noise. Too much flash. And phony flash, at that. The dry air made his eyes itch.

Dane bypassed the general check-in desk for the VIP desk. He'd reserved a two-bedroom suite (a hot tub had been an option Dane passed on). They negotiated the slot machines without falling into temptation and made the ascent to the tenth floor. In the suite, a large window took the place of one wall and offered a view of the desert. Mountains in the distance completed the picture. No balcony this time, but Dane didn't mind.

Nina said, "We can unpack later. I want to try the steak-house downstairs."

"Are you nuts?" Holly said. "How can you eat? If Thorne sees us just lazing around—"

"You can't fight on an empty stomach," Nina said. "And Momma needs her nourishment."

Holly put her hands on her hips and said to Dane, "You gonna let her waste our time?"

"I don't argue with Momma," said Dane.

Dane split his meal, a rare flat-iron steak with skewer of Peruvian shrimp and Yukon mashed potatoes, and broccoli sprinkled with soy onion vinaigrette, with Nina. Holly kept it simple with fried flounder, fries and slaw.

The menus had had a curious notation, one Dane had also noticed in San Francisco, where the calories of each meal were listed below each menu item. Once was a lone health conscious proprietor, twice was a pattern, and the third time a full-blown conspiracy. Obviously, the nannies of the US—those self-appointed do-gooders on a mission to save people from harming themselves by adding warning labels and taxes to everything—had wielded governmental influence and made the notations standard in an effort to make sure folks didn't eat too much of what was bad for them. Those do-gooders marveled at all their do-goodery and yet went to bed each night knowing that, still, nobody loved them.

Dane didn't pay attention to such trivialities. Paying too much attention to what might be harmful meant restraining one's life. Life was meant to be lived, at full speed, and he meant to live it that way. On his terms.

On the way back, Holly spotted a dress shop and said she couldn't keep borrowing Nina's stuff, which Nina heartily agreed with, so Dane sat in the Diamond Crown Cigar Lounge and burned through a La Galera, jawing with other gents, while the women shopped and, he assumed, argued over every stitch of fabric.

Presently they returned to the suite.

Holly said, "I could get used to traveling with you two. I'm going to try on my new outfits."

She locked the bathroom door. Dane pulled his suitcase onto the bed, unlatched the X-ray proof bottom, and took out his gun.

"Put it back," Nina said.

"What?"

"We've only had one moment to ourselves since we started this thing."

"You're just upset because of the third wheel."

"You think? She has atrocious taste in clothes."

"Stop it."

Dane left the gun on the bed and joined Nina at the window. She turned her back to him. "My shoulders are tense."

Dane kneaded the knots out of Nina's shoulders. She let out a breath. He felt the warmth of her skin through her shirt.

"You have barely said a word since we left Arizona."

He worked his fingers lower down her back. Another breath from Nina.

"Arizona was a little rough."

"What are you—"

Holly came out of the bathroom in one of her outfits. "How do I look?" she said. She smiled big and twirled. "This one's my favorite."

Nina shook her head. "Typical."

"You guys need a moment?"

"A couple, Holly."

"I'll just go to my room then," Holly said, disappeared through the doorway to the second bedroom.

"So?" Nina said.

"Forget Arizona," he said. "Tell me the score."

"We're in enemy territory. Tony Nash is the next man on the list, and we decided he's a bad guy because who else could have sold out Roca and the bunch? He knows we're here or will shortly. Presumably Thorne and Skinner are here too, or will be by the end of the day."

"I don't think we're going to make it out of this one," Dane said.

She inched closer to him. "The odds are against us."

"Uh-huh."

She wrapped her arms around his neck. "There's no back-up."

"Nope."

"We've never had it worse."

"Not at all."

She pressed her body into his. "Doom is such a turn-on," Nina said. "It's just you, me, and that dumb Mexican."

Dane gave her a shove. "Now you've ruined the joke," Dane said.

She laughed. "How do you intend to turn the tables?"

"Use myself as bait," Dane said.

"Ah, yes, let them come after you. The old switcheroo and all that."

"Uh-huh."

"And what will me and what's-er-tits do while you're being captured?"

"Find Tony Nash. See if he lives at the hotel, or if he has a place somewhere else."

"Should be easy enough, I'd think."

"Uh-huh."

"And Steve?"

"Yes, dear."

"Please remember that I look horrible in black."

Chapter Twenty-Five

That evening, Dane wandered the casino, checking out the action. Bars and open lounge areas were spaced throughout each level. Cocktail waitresses buzzed around like flies; the noise and voices reached a level of volume that Dane tried to tune out, but each piercing bit made him wince.

From the lobby side of the floor Dane found a curious site that he watched more than once. As families moved in and cut through the casino to the elevators, the men leading those families all had a uniformity of sorts. Ball caps and goatees, mostly combined with cargo shorts and oversized shirts, which draped over their equally over-sized bellies. When their little sons would gaze at the casino, their fathers would call them "buddy" to get them refocused. Dane reflected on something his father had once told him: "I am not your friend. I am your father." The man had been stern and unyielding in his opinions and instilled in Dane his own sense of discipline and loyalty. Buddies were for bragging about girls. Fathers and sons did not fit in that category. No wonder kids in the US were so screwed up.

He noted the lack of visible security cameras, but pit bosses roamed with eagle eyes missing nothing; players, oblivious to both, carried on without a care.

After climbing to the second floor, Dane watched a 70-something man rake in win after win at a roulette table. The streak started to hiccup when two pit bosses pushed through the crowd, replaced the wheelman with another, and leaned on either side of the table. Eventually the older man's smile faded, and he started to lose, but he kept at it. Dane wished him luck.

Dane turned but stopped when he collided with a big brute in a black suit. "Mr. Dane."

"Yes."

"Come with me. Mr. Thorne would like to see you."

Dane grinned.

That was easy.

Dane entered another two-room suite like his, except this one had the hot tub, currently covered. Thorne sat at the table by the window.

Joe Thorne had put on some pounds since Dane last saw him, going from short and skinny to short and stocky, less hair too.

"Hello, Steve," Thorne said, rising from his chair. He approached with hands in pockets. He dismissed Dane's escort, who left the room. "This is a friendly chat."

Thorne went to a liquor cart against a wall. "Drink?" Dane said yes. Thorne poured three fingers of Seagram's and handed the glass to Dane.

Dane took his drink to a chair and turned it to face Thorne. The tinkling of the ice cubes in his glass made the only sound in the room.

"We had a good time in the old days, didn't we?"

Thorne said.

"Define good time."

"I suppose," Thorne said, "we had better talk business."

Dane kept his eyes on Thorne. Thorne did not blink. He breathed slowly, seemingly unbothered by Dane. Either that's how he felt, or he was really working to control himself, Dane decided.

"What kind of business?"

"We need to stop fighting and work together," Thorne said. "Skinner thinks I'm wrong, which is why he isn't here. What do you think?"

"Let's hear your rap," Dane said.

"I already know that you know I'm working with Tony Nash, so there's no sense pretending. We have Meyer's two pieces of the map, you have one, from Grimmer. If either of us gets Nash's piece we won't have the whole thing. Let's pool our resources and do this right."

Dane swallowed some of his drink.

"I know we haven't seen each other in quite some time and, okay, we didn't part on good terms, and we haven't had the best reunion, but we can put that behind us for the score, right? There's a lot of money buried out there."

Dane downed the last of his drink. "No."

"You won't even think about it?"

"No."

"Do you even know what you're up against? Skinner and I have power behind us that can make even you sweat, and your little girlfriend hide in the corner."

"Tell me who it is. Who's pulling your strings?"

Thorne laughed.

Dane said nothing.

"Well," Thorne said, "that puts us back where we started."

"Did you really expect me to agree? Let my guard down long enough for you to shoot me in the back?"

"Always a drama queen," Skinner said.

Dane reached under his coat for the .45. "Why don't I kill you right now," he said, "and be done with this?"

"Blaze away, but what's my fail-safe?"

Dane let out a breath.

"A hotel room is a lousy place for a gun battle, Steve. We're going to have to call it a draw tonight."

"Looks like," Dane said. He put away his gun.

"But you're making a mistake. What do you think you can accomplish here?"

"You'll know when it happens." Dane stood up. "Anything else?"

Thorne made a dismissive gesture.

"Till next time, then." Dane let himself out.

While Dane spoke with Thorne, Nina and Holly sat at one of the computers in the hotel's office center. It didn't take long to compile a stack of articles about Tony Nash. They found clips from television interviews as well. He was a major player in town and didn't hide the fact, cashing in on his Tom Selleck-after-Magnum good looks. They digested the gossip about his dating life and drama surrounding the construction of the Excalibur, but presently found an interview where he mentioned buying a ranch called the Black Cat, located just outside the city. It was an old ranch with a lot of history. It was not hard to find.

Nina drove while Holly monitored the GPS unit included with the car. Nina had sent Dane a text of where they were going, just in case.

It was a warm night, but they hid their pistols under light jackets anyway. Neither expected action; this trip was for recon purposes only, but it never hurt to go armed. Just in case.

When the GPS said they were within a mile, Nina pulled off the road and parked behind a cluster of rocks. They hiked the rest of the way, shoes crunching on the desert ground, the half-moon lighting the way. A few miles off to the right, the highway continued with the occasional car but most of the traffic consisted of big rigs. The women crested a rise and took cover behind more rocks. On the flat valley below lay the Black Cat ranch.

Holly took out her pistol while Nina removed a small pair of binoculars from inside her jacket. She examined the ranch.

"Nice spread," Nina said. "Lots of grass. Single-story house. He has stables for horses that appear empty, a tennis court, and a small pond."

"Why a pond?"

"There are ducks in the pond."

"Cheaper than dogs, I guess."

"Speaking of dogs," Nina said, "there is a pair of two-legged ones wandering outside the house. Carrying rifles."

"No well-dressed man should be without his rifle."

"Maybe you're not so bad after all," Nina said.

"See anything else?"

"Just some cars. Thorne and Skinner could be here."

"I think the gun crew confirms that."

"Or Nash wants extra muscle because he knows we're here."

"What's that noise?" Holly said.

"Hmmmm?" Nina lifted her eyes from the binoculars and listened. "Truck motor."

"Getting closer."

Chapter Twenty-Six

The truck's headlamps flashed over the top of the rise on their left. The lights hit them dead center but not before they identified gunmen preparing to jump out of the back. Nina started to run while Holly jumped up and fired a rapid succession of shots. One of the headlamps winked out, the windshield popped, and a front tire blew, causing the front of the van to sink down. That didn't stop the salvo of return fire from the driver, which cut the air over Holly's head as she ran after Nina. The gunmen who jumped out of the back returned fire as well.

Holly shouted Nina's name. Nina stopped, turned, and fired her own gun at the shooters while Holly caught up, then started running again. Nina steered them toward the highway.

"Wrong way!" Holly said.

"They might get us before we get to the car! Our best chance is a vehicle already going away from here!"

The ground began to slope upward. Holly tripped and fell. Nina grabbed an arm and helped her up. Holly started running again. Nina's lungs burned from the uphill effort.

When they reached the road, Holly dropped against the slope off the right shoulder and said: "Now what?"

Nina knelt beside her and spotted moving bodies getting closer. She gripped the pistol in both hands and fired a pattern of rounds. One of the gunmen fired back and the slugs kicked up ground around her. Another shot whined overhead.

Nina fired again at a moving shadow and heard a scream.

A blast of bright light from an oncoming car brightened their position. Nina jumped up and ran into the lane, aiming at the driver. The car screeched to a halt.

Nina ran around to the passenger side, yanked the door open, and jabbed her gun at the driver. Then she froze.

Skinner McNab, behind the wheel, grinned. The rifleman in the backseat aimed his submachine gun at Nina's face.

"I don't like your odds, Ms. Talikova," Skinner said. "Both of you get in. Now."

The man who joined Dane for the elevator ride wore a leather coat that dangled below his beltline. The man pressed the button for the tenth floor. The elevator started upward. The low hum of the motor filled the car.

The man pivoted with an auto pistol on the end of which was a stubby silencer.

Dane crashed against the man, grabbing his wrist. The hitman pulled his gun arm closer to his body and started to wedge the pistol between him and Dane.

Dane grabbed at the silencer and twisted; the hitman let out a yell as the bones in his fingers cracked; the gun fired, and the slug smacked into the elevator wall. Dane punched the man, put a hand behind his neck and forced him to bend forward. The gun clattered to the floor. Dane brought up a knee and smashed the killer's face. He let the man fall and picked up the gun. As the hitman groaned and tried to rise, Dane clubbed him with the barrel. The hitman flattened out.

The elevator dinged as it reached Dane's floor. The doors opened. Dane straightened his clothes, buttoned his jacket, and stepped out into the hall. The elevator doors closed behind him.

As he walked down the hall, he checked his phone and saw Nina's text. When he reached the door and pulled out his key card Dane saw blood on his pants where the hitman's face had collided with the assassin's knee. He'd think of a tale to tell the dry cleaner when he—

His phone rang. He looked at the caller ID.

Nina.

He answered. "Yes?"

Nina Talikova blew the bangs out of her eyes. She sat on a wooden chair, arms tied behind her, ankles bound too. Next to her, in a similar chair and also wrapped up, sat Holly. Light from a hallway blazed into the room from the open door. More nighttime blackness lay behind the room's one window.

"You okay?" Holly said.

"Uh-huh."

Skinner McNab entered the room. He left the door open. He examined the two women with shark's eyes.

"Ropes aren't too tight, I hope?" Skinner said.

Nina and Holly ignored him.

"Don't feel like talking?"

"Oh, I feel like talking," Nina said. "It doesn't take a wild imagination to figure out what I'd like to say to you."

Skinner took a long knife from his belt. The thin stainless-steel blade flashed in the reflected light.

"You got some fire in your belly," he said. He slashed at the top button of Nina's top. The button fell away. Skinner sliced off another button, exposing the blue camisole Nina wore beneath. "Why do you women insist on so many layers?" Another swipe, another button gone.

"It's a bit nippy out," Nina said.

Skinner laughed. He stepped back and took a cell phone from another pocket. It was Nina's phone. Skinner pressed a button to activate the speaker function and dialed a number.

"Yes?" Steve Dane said.

"I suppose," Skinner said, "that you are in the company of one of my men?"

"You sent an amateur. Don't worry. He'll wake up in a little while. I'm in my suite."

"Feel a little lonely?"

"Everything is fine here," Dane said. "In fact, you helped me out. I picked up this really expensive hooker and she's going to show me how to do the—"

"Will you ever stop behaving like a frat boy?"

"Would you rather I was a psycho nut like you?"

"I am not a nut," Skinner said.

"They better not be hurt."

"We keep playing games, Steve. We each have something the other wants. Be a sport and trade with me."

"Joe already tried that," Dane said.

"Bring me your map piece or the women die."

"Don't do it, Steve!"

Skinner heard Dane laugh. "That's the best you can do? Forget it, Dick. Go ahead and sweat for a bit. We're not going to organize a trade like last time."

"I have your women."

"They can take care of themselves," Dane said. "Especially Nina. She's a former Russian agent and will give you a real bad time."

"Right now, she's tied up. She isn't going anywhere."

"That's a plus. Gives her a challenge. Don't say I didn't warn you."

Skinner made a sound of disgust and ended the call. He tossed the phone on the carpet and left the room in a huff.

"Good ol' Steve," Nina said.

"He's going to leave us here?" Holly said.

Nina laughed. "Holly, you have a few things to learn yet."

Chapter Twenty-Seven

Dane needed transportation to get to Nash's ranch, but Nina had taken the car. Wonderful. Dane stood before the room's big window and considered his options. He could steal a car, but hot-wiring new cars took more effort than he wanted to spend, and those cars might come equipped with a tracking chip, so he'd need an older car. But an older car might break down along the way. Even an older car might have a tracking chip, so no dice on that option. He set out his .45 and cleaning kit on the table and cleaned his gun, loaded spare magazines, and thought about it some more. Then he dressed in dark clothes and a dark jacket and went downstairs to the small branch office of Enterprise, where he had only two compact cars to choose from. At least one of them was blue, which would blend into the desert dark somewhat, but remained less than ideal. Impromptu rescue missions were hardly ever ideal.

He drove the Chevy out of the parking lot and followed the directions printed from a hotel computer. The car didn't have much get-up but it would do. The other car, presumably still accessible from wherever Nina surely hid it, had more power and would be a better getaway car. Not that they would get far. The enemy knew where to find them, after all.

The ridiculousness of the situation finally dawned on Dane, and he laughed as he drove. It wasn't the worst spot he'd ever placed himself, but it ranked among many other poor choices.

Presently he reached the ranch property, parked the car off the road, and slipped under the wooden fence surrounding the place. He didn't trip any sensors or saw any indication that electronic security measures were in place. But that didn't mean there weren't any. He dropped flat to scan the area. The moonlight provided some illumination, but not enough for clear details. The roving shadows near the house were easy to identify. A structure in the distance seemed like a good place to start. But there was no cover to use while he moved, so Dane had to crawl on his belly, digging the edges of his shoes into the ground in order to propel himself forward. It took a long time, and when he came to the duck pond, he stopped.

Three ducks swam in circles; a fourth was out of the water, pecking at the grass. Dane stayed still but it didn't matter. When the fourth duck saw him, it made eye contact and waddled toward him excitedly with its mouth opening and closing, uttering a strange guttural sound of greeting. The duck stopped and stared Dane in the face.

"Beat it," Dane said.

The duck didn't beat it, and soon his three companions left the pond and came forward, pecking the grass every few steps. They surrounded Dane, staring at him.

"I'll turn all four of you into foie gras," he said.

Unless they were explosive ducks or had access to an alarm button, which would have been amazing considering they had no fingers, Dane had no physical fear, but any activity at the pond could rouse the guards at the house. This is the last thing he needed. But as they stared, the ducks made no sound. Dane started to move forward, and the ducks shuffled back, uttering their guttural noises. Dane stopped. The ducks stopped and stared.

"My kingdom for some breadcrumbs," Dane said.

The stare down continued, broken up for moments here and there when the ducks pecked at the grass. One off to the left started to nibble on something and ignored Dane. Dane moved left, the ducks again acting up, but there was nothing else to do. He couldn't sit there all night. They followed him a little, but as soon as he neared the pond they dipped back into the water. Dane stopped and looked around. None of the guards near the house had left their spots. Activity near the pond wasn't alien to them. Fair enough. Dane kept moving, through the open yard of grass, toward the structure about 50-yards away. Looked like horse stables. As he moved closer, he saw no sign of any life. Empty. Terrific. When he finally entered the moon-cast shadow of the building, he rose to his feet. Grass stained the front of his outfit from top to bottom. Dane slipped inside and look around.

The stables were empty, but they hadn't always been that way. Stray hay was abundant, as were tools and saddlery.

Dane started gathering hay and piled it into a stable in the middle of the building. The building had no electricity wired into it, so the three stray oil lamps he found were very welcome. He shook each one. Only the third had any oil left, and he broke open the container and coated the pile. He flicked open his Zippo, stuck the spinner, and set fire to the hay.

Dane ran out of the building to the nearest portion of the

fence. He took out his Detonics Scoremaster and clicked off the safety.

The fire spread slowly, flickering up the walls inside; eventually smoke started to drift across the property, and when the wooden walls finally caught, the flames were visible from the house as well.

Somebody shouted an alarm. Dane watched the guards race toward the fire. Flames spread to the roof. The heat washed over Dane as he lay with his gun in both hands, waiting for the guards to come into range.

There were two of them. They had slung their rifles. One reached the blaze, keeping well back, and shouted into a walkie-talkie. Dane shot him twice. The man dropped mid-sentence. His partner yelled and tried to get his rifle into play, but Dane fired twice again. The second fell near his partner.

Dane jumped up, aware of more activity from the house. Flames and gunshots would wake up the whole crew indeed. Dane ran to the first guard, holstering the .45 and picking up the dead man's rifle along with a spare magazine. He looked at the gun a moment, an M16A4 with iron sights. He ran from the blaze as more figures ran toward it. Nobody fired at him—they were looking at the fire. Dane found a cluster of trees and took cover. One man in particular seemed to be in charge of the crowd as he shouted orders in a commanding voice. Skinner. Dane smiled. Hello, old pal. We meet again. Yes, send the troops in a search pattern to find whoever set the fire because it sure as hell didn't start itself. And then stand there looking at it with your mind clicking because you know I'm here and you know I'm not leaving without Nina and Holly.

The dry wood produced a thick cloud of smoke that wafted across the property, obscuring everybody's view.

Now! Dane aimed at Skinner and fired once. Skinner fell, but not as if he'd been hit. Skinner hit the ground, rolling, shouting orders. A miss. Dane flicked the selector switch to full-auto and fired two long bursts, shifting his aim from left to right. The smoke was thick enough that he could barely see his targets, but that didn't matter. They couldn't see him either and they'd see even less of him while trying to avoid his shots.

Dane jumped up and ran for the house, reloading on the way, heading for the back where there was a patio and pool with outdoor furniture placed where one places outdoor furniture on the patio when one has such things to place somewhere. Dane grabbed a chair and hurled it at the sliding glass door. The crash echoed across the property. Dane rolled inside, coming up on a knee, sweeping the rifle's muzzle around the room. As he stood up two gunmen entered from a hallway. Dane fired, dropping the first one. He fired again as the second returned fire. The gunman's blast went wide while Dane's carefully aimed burst stitched his opponent from chest to throat.

Dane was on his feet and running before the second gunman hit the floor. Skinner and his men would keep searching the property, but a detachment was no doubt racing to the house. Dane moved as fast as he could. It was a large house, many rooms. The open areas—kitchen and dining room—were empty of other shooters, but Dane now heard somebody outside shouting commands. They were surrounding the place. Dane started opening doors. Closet. Garage. Bedrooms. When he opened the third bedroom door, he found Nina and Holly tied up.

"Did you stop for coffee on the way?" Nina said.

Dane slung the rifle and used a knife to cut the women loose.

"We are surrounded," he said, "and outnumbered, but I think I know a way out."

Holly rubbed her wrist. "Which is?"

"You two need some guns first."

"Any sign of Nash?" Nina said as Dane led them back the way he'd come.

"He's probably in a panic room. Rich guys all got panic rooms for times like this."

"Of course," Nina said. "Commando raids are as regular as the mail."

They found the two gunmen Dane had shot. Nina and Holly helped themselves to the rifles and spare ammunition. Dane watched the patio. He saw something move and fired two shots, but no return fire came his way.

"Now what?" Nina said.

"Garage."

Chapter Twenty-Eight

Skinner deployed his men in a crescent pattern to cover the exits.
Dane and the women had to come out sometime.

Skinner lay flat on the ground, propped up on his elbows, a loose grip on his own M16A4. There had been shooting inside, but he knew Dane still lived. Otherwise the pair that had remained behind would have come out.

Skinner wiped his sweaty right hand on his jeans.

And then Nash's silver Mercedes crashed through the garage door and sped across the grass. A dozen guns turned on the car, orange flame flashing from muzzles. The Mercedes soon resembled Swiss cheese as bullets punctured body panels and shattered every window. When the tires exploded, the car stopped but the engine still ran, the rear wheels gouging the ground, kicking up a temporary geyser of dirt, and catching the car in a rut.

Only Skinner did not fire. He kept his rifle pointed at the garage. He knew what his men would find when they reached the car: empty seats and a broken broom handle or some other stick wedged between the driver's side and gas pedal. Dane would speed out in Nash's other car while attention was focused on the Mercedes.

"You'll be dead before you learn any new tricks, Dane," Skinner whispered.

Nothing from the garage.

Skinner frowned.

The stables still burned. Smoke continued to drift but it wasn't too bad where Skinner lay. He looked at the burning building.

"Maybe you did learn something new," Skinner said. He leaped up and ran across the grass, around the back of the patio, and stopped. The three men he'd placed there lay on the ground. Shot dead. Spent shell casings littered the grass.

Skinner turned and looked in the distance past the burning stables. While everybody had been shooting the Mercedes, Dane and the women had run out the back. Their engagement with his men guarding the patio had gone unnoticed over the other gunfire.

Skinner took off in a sprint, plowing through the thick smoke. His eyes stung and he felt heat from the flames, but he did not stop until he reached the wooden fence at the edge of the property.

"Dane! Come back and fight!"

A muzzle flash winked in the darkness. The bullet whistled high over Skinner's head. The crack of the shot followed.

Skinner stood still and stared, seething.

Dane, Nina and Holly returned to their hidden vehicles and drove back to town.

Dane knew that overall the situation as-is could not continue. Dane thought up a scenario that seemed ridiculous but would move them all to the next stage, assuming he survived. Perhaps he'd be the one who needed to be rescued next. Stranger things had happened.

The three entered the hotel separately, each using a different entrance. They looked bad enough as individuals, but three people walking together who looked like they'd been crawling through the mud would surely attract unwanted attention. Not that the enemy didn't know them already, of course. To Dane the precautions seemed silly, but old habits and all that. Proper tradecraft wasn't something one could just toss aside when one found it convenient to do so.

Dane reached the room last. When he entered, he stopped in the doorway. A large man in a dark suit stood in the center of the room, holding a pistol.

"Again?" Dane said.

Nina said: "Steve, this is Bill. From hotel security."

"Hello, Bill from security." Dane shut the door. That's when he saw the other two men, dressed just like Bill, standing near the couches. Nina and Holly sat on the couches with their hands in plain view.

"I don't want trouble," Bill from Security said. "Mr. Nash would like to speak with you, Mr. Dane."

"He couldn't ring me after breakfast tomorrow?"

"He's on his way. He'd like you in his office when he arrives."

"Needs time to get out of the panic room, right?"

Dane went to the dresser and poured a slug of bourbon into a glass. He drank it down and examined Bill and his companions. "Just the three of you?"

"We come well equipped," Security Bill said.

"Just like a luxury car," Dane said. "What kind of gas mileage do you guys get? Combined, I mean."

"Stop fooling around and come on."

"Do me a favor and put the gun away, like a good chap," Dane said. "Let's do this politely. Ladies, I shall return.

Please don't trash the place."

They led Dane down to the lobby to a door behind the VIP check-in desk and along a lighted hallway to an elevator.

The elevator took them up a few floors. The doors rumbled open and the security men escorted Dane into a large office. A sitting area on one side, conference table on the other; straight ahead, behind a desk, sat a man Dane guessed was Tony Nash. The low lights produced a glow throughout the room.

Bill dismissed his two helpers, who stepped back into the elevator. As the doors closed, Bill led Dane to the desk and Tony Nash stood.

Behind Nash was a large window, not unlike the one in Dane's suite, which offered yet another city view. Dane was bored with the view.

Nash identified himself but did not offer to shake hands. Good enough for Dane. He might have snapped the other man's wrist. Dane took the empty chair in front of the desk and Nash told Bill to go back downstairs. Nash did not speak again until the guard left.

"Belated welcome to Vegas."

"Uh-huh."

"I like your style, Mr. Dane. I hope we can resolve this situation."

"We're resolving things here and there, like at your place tonight. Where was your panic room?"

"My what?"

"Where were you hiding during the fight? Do you have a secret room hidden behind a bookcase or something?"

"I was under the bed."

Dane laughed. "Delightful. I never would have looked there. But I wasn't looking for you, actually."

"Will it help if I give you my piece of the map?"

"Now why would you do a silly thing like that?"

"I have been reevaluating my arrangements with Mr. Thorne. Perhaps he has outlived his usefulness and I should join forces with you."

"You're admitting you betrayed Roca and Wexler?"

"It makes no sense to hide that now."

"And together," Dane said, "you expect we'll gather the treasure, split the money, and live happily ever after?"

"We would split the money, for sure."

"What kind of reputation do I have," Dane said, "that you people think I'd participate in anything related to human trafficking?"

"You know about that?"

"I know a lot of things, Nash. Funny how life works, isn't it? You spend all your time chasing a dream and when you get there it's so disappointing you need another dream to justify your continued existence.

"You seem to forget that a friend of mine got killed because of information you gave the enemy. That's what started this whole thing. If you hadn't killed Tom, maybe we wouldn't be talking. But you did."

"I didn't kill him."

"You're responsible. Don't give me any situational ethics garbage."

Nash tapped a finger on his desk a moment.

"I wouldn't make a deal with Thorne, either," Dane said. "He simply wanted to team up. You want to rub him out. You're worse than he is."

"I can have you killed right now."

"And my lady friends would burn this place to the ground. Tony, we know all about you. You couldn't run far enough. But, please, don't let that stop you."

The two men stared at each other a moment.

"We're at a stalemate, then."

"On that I agree. We can't sit here having a staring contest or telling dirty jokes, but we need to move the plot along, so here's an idea. You give Thorne and me a private room and a deck of cards, and we'll draw for the map pieces."

"Are you serious?"

"One side will get the whole thing," Dane said, "and then we'll have some fireworks. Maybe it will end there, or maybe one side or another will get away, and we'll move on to the next phase. Seriously, Vegas isn't that exciting, and if we start boring the audience, they'll find a TV show to watch and we can't have that."

"I don't like TV," Nash said. "Five-hundred channels and nothing to watch."

"No kidding. What about the room?"

"I'll arrange it."

"You'll have to convince you-know-who, but he used to be a sporting man so maybe he'll get a kick out of the idea." Dane rose from the chair. "Good night, Mr. Nash. I'll find my way back down, thanks."

"You indeed have style, Mr. Dane."

"I'm from Iowa, that's where style was born."

Chapter Twenty-Nine

Nina rolled over to rest a hand and her chin on Dane's chest.

"Do you think they'll bite?" she said.

"Silly not to," Dane told her. He pulled up the sheet and comforter to cover her shoulders. She snaked her legs around him.

"Can we match the artillery?"

"Nash won't use his own people. They're rent-a-cops, not killers. That narrows it a little."

"I'm not sure about this."

"Neither am I. But if we can win, we're on our way."

"Your arrogance or your confidence—I am not sure which is worse—will get you killed someday."

"And you look horrible in black, I know."

"What if we did it this way—" and she told him her idea. Later the following afternoon, they visited a nearby electronics shop for the equipment required for the night's activity.

Dane and Thorne sat across from one another at a large poker table. At the head of the table sat a dark-haired dealer with black-framed glasses. He quietly shuffled a deck of cards.

"Looks like I have you outnumbered," said Joe Thorne. Dane only smiled.

"I suppose you have a plan?" Thorne said.

"Your knees are knocking because you actually think I do," Dane said.

The dealer shuffled the cards once more. Thorne cut the deck. Dane glanced at Skinner, who stood over Thorne's left shoulder. They brought along four shooters, all of whom carried pistols concealed under coats. Dane couldn't take them all alone. He didn't think he'd have to.

Dane sat alone. Under his jacket was a small microphone that fed the room's conversations to a receiver monitored by Nina, off site in the car.

The room Nash had donated for the event was part of a second wing of the hotel, used primarily for conferences and banquets with its own entrances and exits. White walls, red carpet—the colors of the ace of hearts. Dane wondered if that had been intentional.

The dealer signaled that he was ready. Dane said: "Simple high card draw. Best of three."

Thorne produced two slips of paper, the edges ragged, from an envelope and set them on the table. Dane did the same with his piece.

"Let's play cards," Thorne said.

The dealer slapped a card face down in front of Thorne, then Dane. They flipped the cards at the same time.

Dane: Ace of hearts.

Thorne: Ten of clubs.

The dealer collected the two cards and set them to his left.

"One for you," Thorne said.

Skinner jumped in. "You think we're going to walk away if you win?"

"Of course not," Dane said. "You would disappoint me terribly if you did."

"Cool it, both of you," Thorne said.

"Next card," Dane said.

The dealer flipped the first card.

Dane: Six of hearts.

Thorne: Eight of spades.

"One to go," Dane said.

Thorne smiled.

The cards dropped.

Dane: Queen of clubs.

Thorne: Nine of hearts.

Dane put the map pieces in Thorne's envelope and stowed it inside his jacket with the map piece he already had. Joe Thorne pressed his lips together. "Wow."

Dane rose. "You're welcome to try something but I have insurance of my own."

Somebody jammed the cold tip of a gun into Dane's neck. Dane turned his head. "And here we go."

One of the shooters took Dane's Detonics while Thorne helped himself to the envelope and Dane's map piece.

Thorne said, "No shooting in the hotel."

"We got a spot picked out," Skinner said.

Thorne issued instructions and the shooters led Dane out of the building. The cool night air touched the sweat on Dane's face. Where were the girls?

The four men loaded Dane into a car. Two sat beside him in the back while the remaining two hopped in front. Dane took a second look at the man in the passenger seat. A bandage covered his nose. The man turned and glared at Dane. "Remember me?"

"My knee does," Dane said.

The driver started the car.

The man on Dane's left had the .45 tucked into the waistband of his trousers. Dane said, "I want my gun back."

The man laughed.

Holly started the car. She did not turn on the headlights. She followed the other vehicle onto the street and once mixed with other cars switched on the lights.

Nina checked the load on her Smith & Wesson and put it in her lap. From her purse she took a second gun, her back-up Glock, and confirmed that it too was loaded.

Holly accelerated to keep the goons' car in view, swinging around other cars, the punch of the Ford's V8 forcing Nina back into her seat.

"What's the plan?" Holly said.

"They'll have to go outside city limits. When they do, we'll make our move. Keep that right foot limber."

"Check."

Nina had to admit the two of them had been getting along much better since their escape from the ranch, but Nina still did not fully trust the other woman. Call it woman's intuition. Call it a sixth sense. Whatever it was called, Nina felt it.

But she had no choice now. Steve was in trouble. Nina's heart raced. She controlled her breathing and focused her mind on the task. The idea of losing him put her on the verge of panic and panic had to be fought just as hard as the enemy. They had planned for this, but that didn't settle her mind.

The goons kept to city streets and eventually cleared town limits. A few other cars kept Nina and Holly from being obvious, but soon traffic thinned to the point that the ungodly knew they were being followed.

Nina powered down her window and unlatched her

seatbelt.

"Get on their back quarter."

Holly pressed the gas pedal and the car leapt forward with a burst of power.

"When the tire blows," Nina said, "hit the brakes."

Nina slipped through the open window, sitting in top of the door, clutching her pistols. The car drew up on the driver's side of the goons' car. The other car began to speed up. Holly increased speed. Nina fired the pistol in her right hand, then the one in her left. A few of the ejected shell casings, propelled by the rushing air, smacked her in the face. She ignored the hot sting. Her rounds punched through the trunk, rear quarter panel, the pavement. Eventually a round hit the back tire. The tire exploded. Holly hit the brakes. Nina braced her body so she wouldn't be flung forward.

The tire unraveled and pieces of rubber flew through the air; the steel wheel dug into the pavement, an arc of sparks flying high. Then the car started to spin.

Chapter Thirty

As the car spun, the goons grabbed for a handhold. Dane shoved his bodyweight at the man to his right, sending an elbow strike into the man's face. The goon's head slammed against the window, cracking the glass, and he slumped down, out cold.

The car screeched across the lanes and jolted once it left the road but stayed upright. When they came to a stop, Dane leaned toward the man on his left, grabbing an ear, twisting. The man screamed. Dane snatched the Detonics and shot the driver through the head. The man in the passenger seat, straining against his safety belt, tried to bring his own gun up.

Dane said, "You don't know when to quit, do you," and shot him too.

The man whose ear he held kept screaming. Dane smashed the .45 on the back of his head twice. The man stopped screaming.

Dane unlatched his belt and crawled across the body to the door and let himself out.

Nina reached him before he had his feet on the ground.

"Got a boo-boo?" Nina said.

"Nothing a shower and a drink won't cure."

They piled into the car. Holly drove off.

Nina said, "If you're nice, I'll help you clean up in the shower."

"I heard that," Holly said.

"Behave, my dear," Dane said from the back seat. "The child will have nightmares."

Thorne and his remaining crew had not lingered. By the time Dane, Nina and Holly returned to Nash's ranch, only two shooters were still there. Nina and Holly quietly, so as not to disturb Nash, took care of them while Dane slipped into the house and walked down the quiet hall to Nash's private office. He sat in Nash's chair, clipped the end of a Montecristo, and lit up. He removed the .45 from under his left arm and placed it on the desktop.

Another hour ticked by. Dane did a lot of thinking. About his mother. About the words he shared with Skinner while in a jail cell in Arizona. By then Dane had tapped a pile of gray ash onto the top of the big oak desk. He was about to add to the pile again when the door opened, and Nash entered. The other man froze.

"You—"

Dane picked up the .45. Nash swallowed as Dane curled a finger around the trigger.

"Close the door. Don't bother shouting for your men because my people have already taken care of them."

Nash pushed the door shut. "No need for guns."

Dane aimed to Nash's belly.

"I suppose you want me to talk?"

"No, I want you to die."

"But I know things!"

"I don't need you to tell me those things. I'll find what I want in your personal effects."

"I'll split the proceeds straight down the middle. Just you and me."

"Why do you keep thinking I can be bought?"

"Everybody has a price."

"You've already given me something, actually," Dane said. "I've lost some perspective lately, but you helped me get it back. Skinner said I was no different than him and Thorne. We're all savages, he told me. I didn't believe it but couldn't quite convince myself otherwise in all this recent excitement. I felt like a savage. Sometimes I am, but that's okay. I'm the force of good that stops people like you. I don't like bad guys, and I have been blessed, if you will, with the skills and abilities to meet you people head-on. I do it because I can. And I'll take this renewed perspective with me to the next stage."

Nash started to sweat. "Please don't kill me."

"One of these days, you people will stop trying to get away with things," Dane said. "Maybe then I'll have to find honest work. I think I told another thug like you the same thing in Mexico a while back. See how you make me repeat myself?"

"I'm begging you."

Dane fired once. Nash landed on the carpet in a heap. Dane left the desk and stood over the body with smoke trickling from the muzzle of his pistol.

Nina tapped on the door. "Everything all right?"

"We're fine here. You?"

"Found some stuff. Computer, cell phone, etcetera. He was packing to leave."

"Timing is everything," Dane said.

Nash's computer contained notes about who he was working with, a woman named Veronica Ansemi. Nina used the internet to dig up information about her, but there wasn't much other than that she was a gangster's daughter who had inherited her father's syndicate in the beach community of San Isabel. Nash's cell phone showed an entry for "Veronica", but Dane felt it best to not call and torment her. No need to tip off the baddies. Thorne would, by now, know that Dane had escaped. Once again, he and Nina and Holly would be walking into the lion's den. But the internet revealed some other information about Ms. Ansemi: she had a competitor, and where one has a competitor, one has an enemy that somebody else can use as leverage.

Dane did not know anything about San Isabel, but a map revealed it as a town on the upper tip of the California coast.

They made immediate travel plans.

San Isabel, California

San Isabel had no airport, so they landed at the nearest one 50-miles away and rented a car for the remaining journey. The big Chrysler sedan hummed all the way. The trip took a little over an hour, the last leg of which included a winding two-lane road over a mountain. The constant twists and turns almost made Holly car sick while Dane and Nina enjoyed every moment.

Dane slowed once they reached the bottom of the mountain which marked the city limits of San Isabel.

The main strip stretched toward the ocean; the shops and restaurants bore names with ocean themes: Salt Water Café, Mickey's Five-Star Seafood, The Barnacle Book Shop. Closer to the ocean they found a large harbor.

Dane pulled into the Tigershark Hotel and arranged for connecting rooms. The night clerk put them on the third floor and promised a view of the ocean, but when the trio stepped out onto the small balcony, they discovered that in order to see the water one had to lean over the rail and look left.

Nina said, "Could be worse."

Dane and Nina decided to take in some of the night-life but Holly, after the drive, said she was in no mood to join them.

Dane tucked the .45 behind his back. He and Nina visited the night clerk again and asked where they could find a good place to eat with a little sporting action on the side.

"Hap's Steakhouse," the clerk said, "but you gotta have the password to get in the back."

"Which is?"

The clerk charged $20 for the information, but Dane figured it would be worth it.

Chapter Thirty-One

They started with a nice dinner at the steakhouse and Dane had to remind Nina not to rush. They'd go to the basement soon enough. The steps leading to the lower basement brought Dane and Nina to a wooden door, in front of which sat a big man with folded arms wearing a tattered brown sport jacket. He rose from a metal chair and asked for the password. Dane said the words. The big man opened the door and said: "Enjoy."

Calling it a basement wasn't the best description, Dane decided. It was a wide room with a bar and tables and booths. Plenty of people. Their mass of voices blended together. Dane and Nina found a space at the bar and both ordered a martini. Nina opted for Stoli vodka while Dane specified Tanqueray gin.

"What do you think?" Nina said.

"It's a bar. No gambling here."

"Look over there." Nina drank some of her martini, turning her head in the direction she wanted Dane to look.

There were three of them at the table, two men and a woman. A large pot of cash sat in the middle of the table.

The men began laying out cards. The one with his back to Dane scooped the pot toward him and let out a laugh. The man on the left of the winner cashed what chips remained and left the table.

"There's your sporting action," Nina said. "Is this the best this town can do?" She frowned. "Do you see what I see?"

"I do."

"Never say that."

"You know what I mean."

The woman at the table, a redhead, matched the pictures of Veronica Ansemi that they had seen on the web.

"What do you want to do?"

"Let's play some cards," Dane said.

Nina followed her man across the floor. He planted a hand on the back of the empty chair. The redhead, who had been gathering the loose cards, looked up.

Dane said, "May I join?"

"The lady, too?"

"She's my good luck charm."

"Buy-in is two-hundred," the woman said, tapping the cards together. She had very dark brown eyes and wore a bulky sweater with a dark green skirt.

Dane pulled a roll out of pocket and peeled off a pair of C-notes. She took the money. Dane sat and scooted close. Nina began kneading his shoulders.

The redhead introduced the other man. Vic Healy was very big with a bald and dented head. His hairy arms sported tattoos near each elbow.

"Five-card stud," the woman said. "No limit. I'm Veronica, by the way." She smiled with one side of her mouth and began dealing.

They played for two hours during which the bar crowded up and a haze of cigarette and cigar smoke hovered below the ceiling, some of it contributed by one of Dane's stogies. He only won two early hands—after that, Healy or Veronica took the rest. It did not take long to realize the pair had a shakedown going. Presently, Dane pocketed what remain of his money and excused himself.

As he rose, Veronica said, "So soon?"

"I know a rigged game when I see it," he told her. "Don't worry. I won't spoil the party. Part of the code and all that." He and Nina began to step away.

"Hey," Veronica said. "If you want to get it back try the tables at the Sand Shack. Tell them I sent you."

"Don't tempt me," Dane said. He winked and led Nina away.

They were out of earshot when the redhead said to Healy: "Check him out."

The cab dropped them at the entrance of the Tigershark Hotel. Nina waited out front while Dane went across the street to a liquor store and returned with a bottle of Russian Standard vodka.

"A petty poker shakedown seems a waste of time," Nina said. "She runs part of the show here?"

"Maybe they get bored. Do you think our exit was enough to make them interested?"

"Bet on it. Come on. This fresh air is choking me."

Dane checked on Holly who was sitting up in bed watching television. She didn't want a drink. He and Nina entered their room. Nina grabbed cups from the bathroom while Dane opened the bottle. They sat at the table and Dane filled the cups. The Detonics dug into his back so he took it out and set it on the table.

They spent time draining the bottle and eventually

something rattled in the doorknob. A snick and the little lock popped. The guy on the other side of the door didn't have to worry about the chain because he wasn't expecting anybody to be there. When the intruder slid his big body and dented head inside, Dane picked up the .45 and aimed at Healy's left eye.

"Hi," Dane said. "Come on in. You like vodka?"

Healy's left arm twitched toward the doorknob, but his eyes stayed fixed on Dane's automatic.

"Shut the door, Healy."

Healy moved his hairy arm again and shoved the door closed. He moved forward, still watching Dane and the pistol. Nina burped. Healy froze. Dane laughed.

"Can't take her anywhere," he said. He set the gun on his lap. "The bed doesn't bite. Sit."

Healy sat on the bed. His arms dangled at his sides. He said: "You're a good poker player."

"When it's a straight game, yes."

"That other guy who was there before you wasn't any good. We took a lot of money off him."

"Do you really need the game to keep your operation running?"

"It passes the time."

"I knew this town had nothing," Nina said.

"Tell me, Healy," Dane said, "did you come here to look around?"

"You two are supposed to be gamblin' at the Sand Shack."

Nina said: "Ha!"

"The only thing we've done since returning is kill this bottle. What are you looking for?"

"Tryin' to find out who you are. Nobody talks to Veronica like you did. She thinks you're somebody."

Nina said, "He thinks he's somebody too." She cackled.

Dane let out a sigh but kept his eyes on Healy. "Search the room, Healy."

Healy blinked a few times.

Dane pointed the .45 at the other man's stomach. "Search the room, or I'll leave you in a ditch."

Healy stood up and rummaged under the bed, felt under the mattress, checked the pillows, the nightstand. He moved slowly, his brow furrowed as if he had to think three steps ahead. He pawed through the dresser drawers, peeked behind the dresser and spent a few minutes checking the bathroom and closet. He stopped and stood in the middle of the room watching Dane and his gun.

"Guess there wasn't anything to find," Dane said. "You done?"

"Yeah."

"Want a drink?"

"No."

"Don't tell Veronica I was here," Dane said.

Nina yelled: "I was here too!"

The corners of Healy's mouth twitched as if he couldn't decide whether or not to smile. He didn't smile and his lips resumed their previous flat line. He left the suite without saying goodbye.

Dane put the .45 on the table and let out a breath.

Chapter Thirty-Two

"What do you expect to accomplish?" Nina said.

"I don't think Joe is in town. If she knew who we were, Healy would have been sent to kill us."

"That means recovery is probably in progress, and if recovery is in progress, we are wasting our time."

"They don't have more than a few days' head start," Dane said. "Even if they have dug up the goods, they have to bring it back or store it somewhere."

Nina said: "Go get me another bottle, lover."

"You've had enough."

She uncoiled from the chair and lumbered over to him and straddled his lap. She booked her hands around his neck.

"Tell me."

"No."

She grinded against him. "Tell."

"I'll go see Veronica's competitor tomorrow," Dane said. "I think he might like a piece of the action."

"I know what I want a piece of," she said, and pressed her mouth roughly against his.

Dane didn't have to go looking for the redhead's competitor—he came to Dane. Or, rather, his goon did.

As he finished dressing, alone in the suite with plans to join Nina and Holly for a late breakfast downstairs (Nina only had a mild hangover) somebody knocked on the door.

Dane left the .45 on the bed and answered.

A light-haired man in jeans, T-shirt, and windbreaker stood in the hall. "You Dane?"

"Uh-huh."

The man smiled and opened the windbreaker enough to show the butt of an automatic. "Make it easy."

"No suit? You seaside gangsters are sloppy."

"Very funny. Car's waiting, come on."

Mark Keller, seated in the back office of an ice cream shop, stood up from behind his desk. Blond hair, black suit, white shirt, black tie.

"That's more like it," Dane told him. "You look like a gangster."

"I'm a working man," Keller said. He dismissed Dane's escort and invited Dane to sit.

"Greetings," Keller said. "My name is Mark Keller and I heard you smarted off to Veronica Ansemi last night. I had to meet you. Nobody talks to Veronica like that."

"And you are the competition."

"You already knew that, Mr. Dane. Like you knew you were playing a rigged game. I wanted to get to you before she did. Drink?"

"Sure."

Keller produced a bottle of Bacardi from a bottom drawer. He poured two glasses. The glasses looked a little dusty but Dane made no comment.

"To crime," Keller said.

They drank. "I forgot how good straight rum tastes," Dane said.

Keller smiled. "What brings you to the beach?"

Dane began with, "I got a tip from a connection in Kansas City about antiquities smuggled out of Iraq," and went into a rap about wanting to offer his services as a fence. He wanted the chance, he added, to get a higher price for the boodle than whoever Veronica had already contacted.

"That's Veronica's gig," Keller said. "I look on with envy."

"I know that," Dane said.

"You talk as if it's already my project."

"We could make it your project."

Keller leaned forward with his elbows on the desk. "Tell me more."

"I can make some moves and get the stuff, but I'll need extra hands. You do the financing. My people and I grab the loot and move it for you. We make it look like an outside job."

"You're very bold."

"I don't believe in taking pies out of the oven half-baked."

"I guess not. Well, now I have things to think about. Go enjoy yourself and I'll find you if I want to talk more. Tell the girl up front to load you up a pound of salt-water taffy. We make the best in town."

And they did. The best Dane had ever eaten, anyway, and he was unwrapping his third piece and enjoying the salty breeze when a car pulled to the curb and Healy leaned his dented head out the window.

"Jump in back."

Dane climbed in and Healy drove off.

"What's up?" Dane said.

"Veronica wants to see you. That taffy from Keller's place?"

"Are you watching me on video or something?"

"Gimme a piece. I love that stuff."

Dane gave him a piece and Healy took off the wrapper with his teeth.

They left the town limits and began an uphill drive. Healy threw the car into the curves with gusto. While the side of the mountain was on one side, nothing shielded the edge of the road on the other side. One slip and down they went, but Healy drove as somebody who knew the route so well there was no risk.

The road leveled off at the oval-shaped driveway of a two-story home. Healy stopped the car and the two men went into the house. A curving staircase on one side, rooms on the other. Out of one of the rooms emerged Veronica Ansemi, decked out in black jeans and a too-large T-shirt. Another curve-killing outfit, Dane thought. She crooked a finger at Dane. Healy went back outside and Dane joined the redhead in the library.

Books lined the walls on shelves that reached halfway to the ceiling. A large window showed an ocean view stretching to the other side of the world.

Veronica told him to take a seat on the couch while she moved to a drink cart. "What's your poison?"

Dane saw a bottle of Maker's Mark and asked for that. She brought Dane his glass and sat on the other end of the couch and crossed her legs.

"I hear you met Mark. Did he offer you a job?"

"Actually, we talked about hijacking the antiquities you're recovering."

"That's not very nice, Mr. Dane."

"Call me Steve."

"If you think you can take that from me, you're braver than I thought."

"Or stupid."

"That too."

"I have a connection that will pay more than you've already arranged for," Dane said. "You might as well have the same opportunity."

She pressed her lips together and nodded. "Or," she said, "I can have you shot."

"You won't do that."

"I won't?"

"I'm too pretty to shoot. You'll see me in your dreams and wonder what kind of lover I might have been."

She opened her legs a little. "What would your good luck charm say if I gave you access the blessings?"

Dane laughed. "There's that."

She crossed her legs again. "Finish your drink and let's take a walk."

Chapter Thirty-Three

Steps carved into the mountain on one side of her property stopped at a flat section that offered a bird's-eye view of the crashing waves. Dane stood beside the redhead, admiring the scenery. The salty breeze was colder here than in town but neither seemed to mind.

"Would you like to kill a man for me?"

"Say that again," Dane told her. He had heard her clearly, but it wasn't a question he'd expected. She asked it as if she were asking him to pick up milk on the way home.

"I need somebody removed from the land of the living."

"Why me?"

"You can't be connected to my outfit. I need to keep my side of the street clean."

"Uh-huh."

"Do this and we can talk some more. Call it an audition."

"Who's the victim?"

"A jackass who used to work for me," she said. "He tipped the Feds to a few things. Nothing came back on us because they only got the small people, but I need to set an example."

"This guy in town?"

She nodded. "He thinks he can make a deal with Mark."

"Tell me where he is and I'll check it out," Dane said.

"You'll do it?"

"I said I'll look."

"Ten grand. And I'll find a spot on the team for you."

Dane wondered if perhaps Thorne and Skinner had never found an opportunity to mention him or if they figured they had left him so far behind that he had no hope of catching up. When the pair returned from wherever they had gone, his presence would be a nice surprise.

At least that is how the picture appeared. Dane wasn't going to put his eggs in that basket, but he saw no way to finish this except to go all in.

He said: "Consider it done."

Dane returned to the hotel where he found the girls out on the balcony.

"Where did you go?" Nina said.

Dane lit a cigar and told them all about it.

"You're seriously going to shoot this guy?" Holly said.

"Of course he is, dear," Nina said. "For him there's a block of ice where normal people have a brain."

"I don't know what I'll do," Dane said, ignoring Nina entirely as he smoked his cigar. "You can bet I'll be watched the whole time."

"Which means we watch you, too," Nina said.

Dane blew a stream of smoke. "Absolutely."

"Could this be a trap?"

"If Veronica wanted me dead, her people had plenty of time to do it today." Dane puffed his cigar. "But I still want you two covering me."

"It's a trap, trust me," Nina said.

"Deep down I know you're right."

Holly said, "Then why go through with it?"

Dane grinned through a cloud of smoke. "Because we're going to have a good time springing the trap and using it against them, that's why."

Veronica had called the place a shack, but it was really a two-room cottage in a small neighborhood about a block from the beach. Dane drove up and down the street twice. He saw nothing but normal activity. Lights burned inside other homes, couples walked hand-in-hand, kids played. He parked a few doors from the target and watched the cottage. The lights were on in there, too. Dane left his car and walked to the porch. He rang the bell but nobody answered. When he gave the knob a twist, it turned, and the door squeaked open.

Dane took out his gun and entered. The television blared from across the room and the target sat in a reclining chair. A boxing match played on the screen. Dane paused. The man in the chair did not move.

Dane called to the man. "Hey."

No response.

Dane frowned as a realization dawned.

He put away the .45 and went to the chair. The man was missing part of his face because of the bullet that had been fired into it, and the remains of that missing half decorated part of a wall and the carpet.

Dane heard a horn—three short bursts. Nina's signal.

He ran for the door but stopped as Healy and another goon hustled up the walk. They yelled for him to stop. Dane bolted the other way. The goons reached him before he could get to the patio door and Healy pulled Dane's arms behind him. Dane twisted out of the grasp, swinging and kicking, the blows connecting to Healy, who went down hard. The other had a Taser out but Dane grabbed the goon's wrist and twisted as the bolts flew. The prongs landed on the carpet. Dane slammed a fist into the man's mouth and the goon fell back. Healy leaped up from the carpet. His wide swing connected with Dane's face. Dane fell back against the patio door but didn't crash through. He jumped up as Healy converged, but Healy swung a handgun against Dane's head and Dane fell down again.

Dane awoke in the back seat of a big Lincoln sedan. Healy's skinny partner sat next to him holding a gun. The door to Dane's left was open. A man stood outside looking at him.

Mark Keller.

"Wakey, wakey," Keller said. "Welcome to my cabin in the woods where nobody is going to hear us kill you."

Dane blinked a few times.

"You made a big mistake, Dane," Keller said. "Veronica and I are already working together. Nice try, though."

Healy joined Keller and dragged Dane out of the car. Skinny left the car and joined his partner. Healy dragged Dane across the dirt yard and dropped him near the edge of the trees.

"Veronica and I wanted to string you along some more," Keller said, "but you're moving awfully fast, and our boss in Moscow is tired of all this fooling around."

Dane sucked in a breath.

Moscow?

"I've never personally dug a grave before," Keller continued, "but I dug yours, Dane. Took a while, that's why we needed to send you on that little errand. But I got it done. It's fairly deep. I think you'll like it."

Dane glanced around. Two more gunman armed with

submachine guns stood nearby. They had all come in two cars, which were parked in front of the A-frame cabin. Healy reached for a handful of Dane's hair, wrenched up his head.

"We came out on top, smart guy," Healy said. "Think about that when we shoot you."

"Too bad, Healy."

"Why?"

"I liked you."

Healy let go of Dane's head. Dane's left leg snapped out, connected with a knee or shin. A scream followed. Healy folded against the impact. Dane rolled Healy on top of him, the surrounding gunmen shouting for Healy to get out of the way. Healy pushed up from Dane, drew a fist back. Dane clamped his hands on either side of Healy's head and dug both thumbs into his eyes. Warm, wet fluid rushed down Dane's wrists and Healy screamed. Dane snatched a .38 from Healy's belt, letting the other man's weight fall against him. Skinny and Keller scattered. Dane rolled a little to the left and shot the first sub-gunner in the chest. The remaining sub-gunner ran for one of the cars. Dane fired twice. The gunner hit the ground face-first.

Dane rolled the still-screaming Healy off him. He jumped up, took a few steps, stumbled, crashed. Pistol shots nicked the ground. Dane rolled into the sharp brush at the edge of the clearing. Gasping, gritting teeth, he rolled to a tree stump and let out a loud cry. He lay gasping and watched Healy rock side-to-side with hands covering the mess where his eyes once were. He was still screaming. Dane aimed the .38 and fired once. Healy stopped screaming.

Chapter Thirty-Four

"I think we lost them."

Nina wasn't so sure and told Holly so.

"We can't stay here for long," Holly said. "Either we have or we haven't. Considering nobody else has come into this garage, I think we're safe."

Healy and Skinny had been waiting for Dane, but the opposition had other goons watching Nina and Holly too. Nina managed to evade them, it seemed, but she wondered how long they could indeed wait at their present location. The multi-level parking garage adjacent to a commuter train station was currently empty except for them.

"What should we do now?" Holly said. Nina's tiger eyes darted back and forth as she scanned for threats while still sitting behind the wheel. Her face was a mask of concentration and Holly wondered if her words broke through.

"Do you have spare ammunition?"

"Two magazines," Holly said.

"I have two as well." Nina tapped the steering wheel. She scanned some more, especially the darkened areas outside the lighted garage where the train tracks were. She had parked in a corner to avoid anybody sneaking up from behind, but a quick-moving team would know how to take advantage of any openings along the structure.

"You want to go and shoot somebody?" Holly said.

"Let's go and shoot Veronica Ansemi."

Nina started the car.

"You want to go to her house?"

"If we've dodged her goons, they're busy looking for us, and that means they aren't at her place, and that means we may be able to get in and find out what's happened to Steve."

"I'm sure he got away. Let's try the rendezvous point and see if he's waiting."

"We're at the rendezvous point, honey."

Holly said: "Oh."

Nina drove out onto the street.

Dane looked at the cabin. Skinny and Keller were hiding behind the porch railing, shielded by the hedgerow. The snub-nosed .38 wasn't made for long-range work so Dane didn't want to waste bullets trying to get them. He scanned the lot. The cars. The bodies. The cars would make good cover and the dead soldiers had submachine guns.

Dane pushed to his feet, and all he managed was a fast shuffle into the clearing, kicking up dust along the way. Skinny and Keller opened fire. Once, twice, then two shots together. None struck. Dane reached one of the cars. A shot smashed the upper corner of the roof. Dane scooted to the driver's side, keeping low as he went from there to the front bumper. A dead gunner now lay only a few feet away, and Dane scrambled toward the corpse. Propping up on the dead man's chest, Dane aimed the Beretta M12 submachine gun at the house and let go a salvo that almost shook the weapon from his hands.

Return fire from Keller flew wild. Skinny leaped off the porch and Keller followed him around the side of the house.

Dane grabbed two extra magazines from the dead gunman. His arms shook as he tried to keep the sub gun aimed at the house. He ran back to the stump. It seemed like the only safe place for now.

Nina followed the winding road up into the hills, found a cut-out, and jammed the car into it. She was well off the road. Holly had to scoot across the front seat to exit on Nina's side, and the two women ran into the brush. The ocean raged in the distance. Darkness surrounded them.

Pistols in hand, they started up the slope of the hill, pushing through the brush, branches and fallen trunks providing obstacles to climb over or go around. Soon they reached a point where they could drop behind cover and examine the grounds of Veronica Ansemi's home.

Lights blazed inside the house; a pair of cars sat in the driveway. Nina counted two guards roaming about, each armed with an automatic weapon and what looked like night-vision goggles with which they scanned the darkened property. Nina and Holly remained low, behind a log, flat on their bellies.

"I don't suppose you brought a grenade with you?" Holly said.

"Not tonight."

"No explosive belt-buckle?"

"Not on this belt," Nina said.

"Will your watch double as a smoke bomb?"

"Not the one I'm wearing," Nina said.

"All we have are pistols against machine guns and

night-vision goggles," Holly said.

"That's it."

"I'll go around the back of the house," Holly said. "Maybe I can cause a diversion."

Nina said okay and clicked off the safety on her Smith & Wesson. Holly moved away, deeper into the brush, and soon Nina lost sight of her.

A guard approached, stopped, made a half turn as he scanned with his goggles. He seemed to look straight at Nina. He stared in her direction and didn't move. She froze, ready to bring up her pistol, but then the guard turned the rest of the way and headed back for the house. Nina raised her gun and set the glowing night sights on the man's back. She took up the slack on the trigger, but then held her fire. She had no silencer on the gun. Nina shifted to lie on the ground against the log while she considered her next move, and her knee bumped something. She looked closer and felt the thickness of a branch. She hadn't played baseball since she was a child, but one never forgot how to swing a bat. She grabbed the branch and waited for the guard to come back.

Dane watched the silent cabin from behind the stump.

Soon the front door opened, and Keller rushed out with a weapon recovered from inside. While Keller ran into the clearing, Skinny fired a sub gun from the doorway, spraying the trees and bushes around Dane. Dane stayed low and listened to the rounds whistle. The flash of Skinny's weapon gave Dane a nice target. He fired the Beretta M12 once and down went Skinny.

Keller reached the black car and ducked near the front fender.

Dane fired a full-auto burst. The front passenger side

tire exploded, that side of the car sinking. Keller appeared around the back end and Dane's next burst stitched a pattern of holes in the fender.

Dane reloaded as rounds split the foliage, struck the stump. Shards of bark peppered his neck. He held back the Beretta's trigger and flame split from the muzzle, sending hot stingers into the back end of the car. Keller let out a clipped yell.

Dane reloaded again, let the dust clear. He couldn't see Keller's body. He rose and hustled over to the car. As he rounded the bumper, Keller lunged from a crouch, swinging his weapon, crashing the butt against Dane's head. Dane fell, rolled, and as Keller closed in, Dane fired the last few rounds in the Beretta's magazine. The slugs punched through Keller's stomach and chest. He fell back against the car, hit the ground, and didn't move any more.

Chapter Thirty-Five

Nina didn't know if it was the same guard, but who cared? She wanted the automatic weapon and maybe his radio. The guard moved softly across the ground, barely making a noise. He scanned the area again as before. Nina flattened as much as she could against the log, clutching the branch. She turned her head a little to better blend in and let peripheral vision follow the guard. He moved past her position and followed the tree line a little further, stopped, and made his way back. He did not linger over her spot this time. His radio crackled. He stopped to listen. Nina heard the transmission but not the words. The man, with a deep voice, responded; as he spoke, Nina moved.

Rising, stepping over the log, Nina planted her foot carefully. The soft ground shifted a little. Closer. The guard's radio crackled some more, and he replied. By the time he finished speaking, Nina swung.

The branch struck the man on the side of the head. The branch snapped in two. The guard let out a grunt as he fell, but when he hit the ground, he rolled a little. Nina stepped closer to swing again. The man rolled away, and she gouged the dirt. The guard rose halfway, bringing up his rifle. Nina swung and smashed his head a second time, dropping the guard flat. Didn't move. She landed on her knees beside him, unclipping the rifle from the sling around his back. She hefted the weapon. It was a SIG SG-552 Commando, a short-barreled automatic weapon. More than adequate. A touch of the safety switch assured her it was in the "fire" position.

Nina grabbed the guard's extra magazines, stuffing them in the pockets of her jeans, and the night vision goggles which she placed over her head and eyes. The area, with a green tinge common to all night vision pieces, was now much clearer. She charged ahead at a low crouch, her focus on the front of the house. The second guard stepped around the building and stopped. Twenty yards ahead. He saw enough to shout an alarm. Nina triggered a burst. The man did not fall. He returned fire. The rounds zipped overhead. Nina dove for the ground, rolling and rising again to fire two more rounds. But the guard was running too, and the shots flew wide.

Nina ran to the right, toward the center of the driveway, where a row of hedges provided lousy cover. Plants won't stop bullets. She hit the ground and low-crawled the remaining distance as the guard fired some more. The shots kicked dirt into her face, crackled across her back. She rolled behind the hedges, leaning out far enough to fire again. This time the guard fell.

An alarm sounded, filling the air with a howl, but Nina stayed put. Two more guards emerged from the front door. Nina fired another string of shots, bringing one down. The other fired as he ran for cover. How many more? Nina remained still and scanned the area. The alarm still blared. No sounds of a fight reached her from the rear of the property, where, presumably, Holly was working; had something happened to her?

Nina spotted the winking strobe of the other guard's rifle. Shots clipped the hedges and pieces landed near her. A little gardening with your gun battle? Nina sighted and fired, shifting her aim a little, uncertain if she scored a hit. The guard fired back and stitched the dirt directly beside her. He'd score sooner rather than later if she stayed in place.

Nina triggered another burst. The SG-552 clicked empty. She buttoned out the magazine and reached for one of the spares, but her pockets were empty. She looked back along the path she had crawled and saw one of them. More than a few feet away. As the guard opened up again, she dashed to the fallen magazine, slammed it into the gun, and turned to fire. The guard was moving toward her. She fired again and the trooper jerked with hits. He landed on his face and didn't get up.

Nina found the other magazine and returned it to another pocket. She turned for the house. An engine rumbled from behind, bright headlights flashing across her. Caught in the open. She swiped off the goggles and fired at the car. The windshield shattered. Four gunmen piled out. She dropped the driver but the passenger sprayed a salvo from his machine pistol. She ran for the tree line, zigzagging, shots going wide but coming terribly close. Her right foot struck something and she tumbled end-over-end into the dirt, the SG 552 flying from her grasp.

Somebody, a woman Nina could not see, shouted, "Take her alive!" and Nina, winded, her left side flaring with pain, rolled onto her back with the Smith & Wesson pistol in hand. The remaining three troopers converged. She fired three times. The man in front fell. The other two kept coming. She fired again and again but neither of the other two went down. She fumbled for another magazine as the Smith's action snapped open, but before she could load, they were on her, one swinging the butt of his rifle into her face.

Dane grabbed spare mags for the Beretta SMG and hopped in the Lincoln. He drove straight to Veronica's. Nowhere else to go now. When he found Nina's car on the access road, he pulled in behind it and killed the motor. Exiting the car, he held the Beretta close as he trudged through the forest.

How long had Nina and Holly been here and had they made any moves? He'd know soon enough. As his boots sank into the damp terrain, he heard a twig snap. He dropped, raising the M12 in that direction. Holly stepped out from behind a tree with her hands up. "It's me, Steve!"

Dane rushed to her. "Where's Nina?"

Holly related what happened in front of the house. "I saw them take her," she said. "I wanted to get back to the car to try and find you."

"Well here I am," Dane said. "Let's go."

Holly led Dane up the hill to the log where she and Nina had used as a hiding place. Dane examined the lay-out ahead of him. The signs of the fight were obvious. Dane eyed the last car to arrive, the one Nina had shot full of holes.

Holly said: "What are you thinking?"

Dane gave her the Beretta. "Cover me."

Dane broke cover and stayed low to the ground, crawling toward the car. He moved behind it, scooting under the body. He found the hose connected to the fuel tank, re-moved his knife and cut the hose. Fuel rushed out. Some of the gasoline dampened Dane's clothes but he moved out from under the car before too much soaked him. The gas pooled on the ground. The smell and the fluid on his body gave him a grim flashback, but he had to put it out of his mind. He needed to rescue Nina. His personal discomfort didn't matter.

Dane opened his Zippo, flicked the spinner, and lit the gas. He ran back to Holly.

"Move it," he said, shoving her in the direction of the house. The car ignited right away. Guards started yelling. Dane and Holly didn't bother with stealth, and stomped through the overgrowth until they were directly across from the house. Through a large window they looked into Veronica Ansemi's study. She was in there alone, pacing. Somebody entered the study, shouted the news of the fire. She spoke something in reply and the gunman left.

"Shoot the glass," Dane told Holly. "Don't hit me."

Pistol in hand, Dane rushed out of the trees to the window. The Beretta chattered behind him. Bullets shredded the glass, the window falling into pieces. Dane leaped through, landing in a tight roll, jumping up to rush Veronica. She screamed. He conked her on the side of the head and she dropped in a heap. He picked her up and dropped her on the couch. Holly slipped through the window.

"I think Nina is in the basement!"

The library door opened again. Two gunmen entered as Dane and Holly opened fire. One jumped out of the way as bullets tore into the second man. Before the first drew his own pistol, Dane shifted his aim and shot him in the left eye. The man fell against the wall and to the floor.

Dane and Holly left the library. There was only one man watching Nina, and Dane used one round from the pistol to clear that obstacle. They returned to the library. The rest of the guards were outside dealing with the burning car with a garden hose.

Nina said, "I need a gun."

Dane found her two guns which he took from the gunmen in the library.

"Ready?" he said.

Holly opened the two front doors and the trio used the doorway for cover as they fired on the men outside.

The fight ended quickly.

Chapter Thirty-Six

"Wake up."

Dane slapped Veronica's face. She moaned. He crossed to the liquor cart, grabbed a bottle of Jameson and poured the whiskey over Veronica's face, her blouse. He propped open her mouth and poured some down her throat. The woman coughed, retched, and sat up. She coughed some more. Dane grabbed one of her arms and dragged her across the carpet until she put her feet under her and stood. She tried to throw her weight against his. He jabbed her belly with the snout of his automatic. They stepped over the body blocking the door.

"Where are we going?"

"Quiet."

"Where are my men?"

"Dead."

Dane took her outside and to the top of the rock overlooking the ocean and shoved her away from him. She turned to face him.

Dane pulled his lighter from the right pocket of his pants. "I win," he said.

"This isn't a poker game, Dane," Veronica said.

"Look who's talking," he said. "You've made your last bluff."

"Go ahead and shoot. Get it over with."

"You don't get off that easy."

Dane flicked the Zippo and touched the flame to her alcohol-soaked blouse. The flame blossomed and jumped into her face. She screamed, slapping her chest. Dane delivered an enraged kick into her stomach and she flew backward over the edge of the rock trailing flame as the crashing waves swallowed her scream.

Dane watched her body burn a moment before the crashing waves eliminated the fire and left only charred remains.

Then he went back into the house.

Papers in Veronica's wall safe, which Dane easily opened when he found the combination in her desk, revealed the assembled map and information on how Thorne and Skinner would reach the location of the stolen antiques. An abandoned mine in Montana. He found some other items, too, but didn't mention those to Nina.

On the way to Montana, Dane called Todd McConn and another former 30-30 associate named Devlin Stone, and asked them to meet him in Big Sky Country. "Bring lots of guns," Dane said, "and anything that goes boom."

McConn and Stone met Dane and the women at a motel, and for a moment the men enjoyed a few laughs. Stone, always quiet, was a little shorter than McConn, with longer hair that covered the tops of his ears. Every now and then he'd brush at either ear but never made any attempt to comb back or even trim the irritating strands. Stone brought the toys: M-4 automatic rifles and LAW rocket launchers. Dane examined each weapon and approved of the gear.

Veronica's notes included what day and time the convoy had departed and when they were expected to return. Dane and Company figured that, since they had flown in, they had a slight lead and could meet the convoy before it reached the buried boodle. The team plotted their ambush point using the map and set out via motorbike to await the arrival of Thorne's convoy.

When Thorne's convoy came abreast of the ambush point, Dane used binoculars to identify Skinner and Thorne and when he gave Stone a thumbs-up, Stone let the first LAW rocket fly.

The big V8 in the Hummer H2 purred as Dick "Skinner" McNab followed the curving road. Joe Thorne sat beside him. Both carried pistols under their coats. Automatic rifles lay on the floor of the back seat; Skinner, out of habit, had a pair of grenades clipped to his web vest. Behind their vehicle was a second Hummer containing four more gunmen; behind the second Hummer trailed two semi-trucks.

Skinner's Hummer bounced over some potholes. He stayed focused on the road while Thorne scanned for threats, and occasionally glanced at the wide open country around them. Summer in Montana meant green hills and blue sky. Montanans joked that the state only had two seasons—winter and road construction—and the convoy had driven through a few such road repair operations, but the highway had been clear of almost all other traffic for the last two hours.

"It would be easy to get lost out here," Thorne said.

"Not if you have a GPS."

"Not what I mean," Thorne said. "I could die out here and be happy."

"With your share of the loot, you can buy a place."

"Might just do that."

"Think Dane is on his way?"

"Probably," Thorne said.

He had not been able to reach Veronica or Mark for three days. Dane could have taken them out and found Veronica's notes. But he would need help, and it would take time to gather his own troops. Thorne had plenty of gunners. His group outnumbered Dane. Dane may have thought he was the best in the world, but even he wasn't dumb enough to take on odds greater than he could handle.

Skinner glanced at the dash-mounted GPS just as a rocket flashed from a cluster of rocks and struck the second Hummer behind them. The shockwave from the explosion tossed them off the road and into a ditch. Automatic weapons crackled. Another rocket blasted a semi into a fireball.

"Where'd he find the rockets?" Skinner said.

Thorne shouted, "We're sitting ducks if we stay here! Floor it!"

McConn fired a second rocket into the cabin of the semi. The resulting blast sent chunks of debris over Dane's position.

The second semi stopped short of plowing through the burning wreckage and while Dane and McConn triggered their M-4s at Thorne's vehicle, Stone fired a LAW at the semi's cargo trailer and more fire and debris joined the fray.

Dane dropped his M-4 for the last LAW. He lined up on the departing Hummer and pressed the trigger. The rocket closed the distance in a flash but not before Skinner wrenched the vehicle out of the ditch. The rocket smashed into the pavement, the blast peppering the back of the Hummer.

McConn gunned the engine of his motorbike. Stone

jumped on his and Dane followed. They put the flaming mess on the road behind them as they trailed the dust wake of the Hummer.

Thorne and Skinner had a good lead, but the motorbikes gained ground quickly. Dane's ears, still a little numb from the start of the fight, hardly registered the chopping sound of his motorbike, and his eyes stung from the trailing dust cloud. More dust clung to his sweaty face, lips, tickled his nose. He twisted the throttle, pulled ahead of Stone and McConn, and eased up along the left rear panel of the Hummer. He took out his Detonics Scoremaster and fired random shots into the vehicle. The back-passenger window rolled down, and Thorne shoved the snout of his rifle through. Dane dropped back as the other man fired. Dane returned fire, the two last rounds in his gun, but missed the back tire. Holstering the pistol, he sped up, leaped onto the motorbike seat, and then flung himself at the back of the Hummer, grasping the rear ladder and hauling his body onto the roof.

The sunroof slid back. Thorne rose through the opening, struggling to get his weapon through the narrow hole. He swung the muzzle Dane's way. Dane deflected the gun as Thorne pulled the trigger. Hot brass ejecting from the gun smacked Dane in the face. Dane balled a fist and punched Thorne once, twice. As Thorne twisted his weapon from Dane's grasp and tried again to shoot him, Skinner swung the Hummer left, right, and back again. Dane tumbled through the air and landed hard on the hot desert ground.

He hurt in places he didn't think it was possible to feel pain. Dane tried to breathe without sucking in sand, but his head felt like it weighed a ton. The hot sun handed out its own punishment.

A shadow fell over him. A motor barked. A voice.

"Come on, Steve."

Todd McConn's voice.

"They're getting away, dude."

Dane moved a little and groaned.

"No time for a nap."

Dane rose on his elbows, put his knees under him.

"Stone's alone out there; let's go. Why are you still on the ground?"

Dane mumbled something that sounded like a curse. He stood up, his arms limp, wavering a little. McConn, still on his bike, scooted forward and Dane climbed on behind him. McConn accelerated away. Dane's stomach lurched.

Chapter Thirty-Seven

Devlin Stone kept well back from the Hummer. With the flat, open desert, it was easy to follow. Especially with the dust trail.

Presently, the Hummer pulled into an opening in a low mountain range, slowing as it came upon the remains of an old mining town. Stone parked the bike against a rock and followed on foot. The Hummer stopped in front of the town church, the wooden building decayed and long past its prime. But the bell tower on the roof would give the enemy the perfect view of the dirt road he, Dane and McConn needed to follow. Stone watched from the cover of another wood building—a single-level—as Thorne and Skinner exited their vehicle and ran into the church.

Forty-five minutes ticked by. Then Stone heard the chopping motor of McConn's bike. He looked back to see both McConn and Dane on the bike. They turned onto the road. Potshots cracked from the bell tower. Stone returned fire. One of his shots struck the bell. The echoing ring bounced between the other buildings and faded fast.

McConn and Dane jumped off the bike and rushed to Stone's position. Dane reloaded the Detonics and sat against the wall a moment. His body tensed and he stifled a grunt.

Stone said: "Have a nice fall?"

"I liked summer better," Dane said. "They're in the church?"

"Yup. I suppose we can wait for a lightning strike or an earthquake. Unless the Good Lord forgot about this place."

"You're a pirate and a blaspheme," Dane said.

McConn jumped in. "They have a three-sixty view up there."

"Uh-huh."

"If we had sniper rifles, we could get them easy."

"If its and buts were candy and nuts," Dane said, "oh what a party we'd have."

Stone said: "I bet your nuts have been pulverized."

"You really know how to cheer up a guy," Dane said.

"What's the plan?" McConn said.

Dane eased around the corner. Thorne and Skinner kept low in the tower, but he saw them behind their rifles.

"They have a good spot but there's a problem," Dane said.

"Which is?" Stone said.

"You found it by accident, Dev. The bell."

McConn laughed. Dane leaned against the wall as he rose to his feet. "When I get close," he said, "ring that bell."

McConn snapped a fresh magazine into his M-4. "Like a John Wayne movie I saw last week."

Dane ran around the corner. His body protested with aches and creaks, but he pushed on. Staying close to the buildings along the street, he had cover if required. But he kept his eyes on the front of the church.

Thorne and Skinner opened fire. Single shots, a burst, the rounds kicked up dust and rocks and splintered wood. Dane clutched the .45. The checkered grips dug in despite the sweat on his hand.

Gunfire behind him. Stone and McConn joining the party. The bell rang...BONG! Again. BONG! A third time. BOOOONG!

Dane sprinted the remaining distance, up the steps, and through the front door.

He saw Skinner McNab first.

Skinner stumbled into the sanctuary from a side door. The echo of the bell filled the room. He raised his submachine gun, but Dane fired first. The slug drilled Skinner right between the eyes. Skinner's head snapped back. His body hit the floor.

"Told you, Skinner," Dane said. He ran up the aisle. Thorne shouted the dead man's name, then fired a salvo from above. The doorway to the steps of the bell tower shattered from the bullet strikes.

Dane knelt beside Skinner's body and tugged a grenade off his web belt.

"Skinner!"

Dane took cover behind a pew, the altar on his right. Christ on the Cross, observing. Déjà vu all over again.

"It's just you and me, Joe!"

"Dane!"

"Sucks, don't it."

"I suppose it's too late to discuss a split?"

"It's been too late for a long time, Joe." Dane left the pew and approached the doorway.

McConn and Stone entered, Dane waving them back;

the pair hustled up the aisle and covered Dane.

"You're outnumbered, Joe. Come down and take your punishment."

A burst of automatic fire filled the doorway again. Dane didn't flinch. He stepped closer.

"You either face me or shoot yourself, Joe."

Dane pulled the pin on the grenade.

Another blast of gunfire, this one cut short. Dane charged through the doorway, up half the steps, and lobbed the grenade upward. Thorne screamed. Dane leapt back to the bottom of the steps and cleared the doorway as the grenade blast shook the walls.

Pistol in hand, Dane raced up the steps to the landing. Finger tight on the trigger. Just in case. He reached the top. Lowered the gun. There was no need for another shot. Thorne's blasted body lay unmoving beneath the bell.

Dane said, "It tolls for thee," and went back to his friends.

They used the Hummer to complete the journey.

Dane turned the Hummer into the property of the abandoned mine. Weeds poked through cracks in the pavement. The weather-beaten buildings, large and small, had missing pieces of trim and broken windows. The trio stopped in front of the mine shaft elevator.

"This will be fun," McConn said.

Stone grunted his agreement.

Stone and McConn pried open the doors with crow bars; the empty shaft welcomed them with a blast of dust and stale air. They turned away, coughing. Dane unloaded Thorne's rappelling gear and the three men prepared for the descent. Their gear included hard hats with attached lights, breathing masks, and goggles. They anchored ropes on the upper portion of the elevator support structure and began the foot-by-foot process of lowering themselves beneath the earth.

More dust choked the interior. They breathed through filtration masks and the lights on the hard hats lit the way, the beams of light resembling powerful spotlights. They could not see any hint of ground below, just a patch of darkness that enveloped them as they moved further and further from the opening at the top. Their boots scraped the metal frame; bits of rock fell from the sidewalls; their heavy breathing overpowered every other sound. Every few feet Dane paused to wipe the dust off his goggles and used a sleeve to remove some of the sweat from his brow. His muscles strained as he fought to remain upright with the rappelling harness tightening against his middle. Gravity wanted to pull him down faster than he wanted to go; one misstep and he would be heels-over-head.

They reached the end of the shaft, which put them on top of the old elevator car. They climbed down and stood on solid earth. Their lights picked out elements from the mine's past, old gear and equipment strewn about, rusting track rails leading into dug-out tunnels. Dane consulted the map and led the way. The three men walked on either side of the tracks, close to the wall. When they reached the side shaft they wanted, they stepped carefully into the opening and continued the advance. When they reached the end of the tunnel a short time later, they froze at the sight before them.

Dane took a route that allowed them to bypass the remains of their ambush and dropped McConn and Stone at their hotel. He told them to stand-by for another twenty-four hours. But he didn't tell them why.

Hands tight on the steering wheel, Dane returned to

Nina and Holly.

As he stepped into the room, Holly said, "It's about time."

Dane had a snappy comeback ready as he shut the door, but what he saw choked off the words: Nina stretched across the bed, tied at ankles and wrists, a gag over her mouth.

Holly stood at the foot of the bed holding her SIG-Sauer against Nina's head.

"Where are the other two?" Holly said.

"I'm alone."

"Good. You know what I want?"

"More than a reward," Dane said. "And this is the way you go about it?"

"Talking to you is like talking to a brick wall. I didn't come all this way just to split a reward. I want the loot. All of it."

Nina made a grunting noise through her gag.

Dane told her, "This is the second or third time you've let yourself get tied up. If you like it so much, I suppose we can add it to our bedroom routine but—"

"Stop!" Holly said. "Give me the map or I'll shoot her."

"And how do you think you'll collect everything?"

"Let me worry about that."

"Did you really love Tom?"

"What?"

Dane moved forward. "Were you with him just to get the boodle or did you really love him? His last thoughts were of you, Holly. I think it was real with him. What about you?"

"Not another—"

Dane lunged and crashed into Holly, forcing her back into a wall. The SIG cracked. Dane punched her and snatched the gun from her fingers as she fell. He turned. The bullet had ripped into the bed where Nina—

Had been.

Nina let out a stream of muffled words. Dane went to the other side of the bed. She'd rolled onto the floor when Dane made his move and lay on her face.

Dane cut the ropes and yanked off the gag.

"Nice move," Nina said. "I told you I didn't trust her. Do I get to see the loot now?"

Dane grinned and helped her up. "Let's take a ride."

PART TWO

Chapter Thirty-Eight

The Rockies were so close, Steve Dane felt like he could reach out and touch the jagged slopes.

The morning chill cut through his jacket as he stood outside the one-story home in a quiet cul-de-sac. It wouldn't be cold for long once the sun fully rose, and the peace of the morning calmed Dane head to toe. Birds chirped. It wasn't a bad place to be after the last few days.

They were in Butte, a small Montana town famous for its copper mining operations. It had been the closest town to where they'd left the Iraqi antiques. They'd left Holly unconscious in the motel. She could fend for herself from now on. If she ever came after them, Dane and Nina had ideas on a permanent solution, but Dane knew her type. She'd run wherever the wind took her and find another sucker.

The home, rented via Airbnb, was the team's temporary base while they planned their next moves. Twenty-four hours had passed since the discovery of the buried antiques, but they had already faded from Dane's mind as he turned his thoughts to the next stage: busting the human trafficking ring for which the money from the sale of the stolen artifacts had been destined.

Dane stood outside the front door and puffed a La Galera cigar while dialing a number on his cell. Phone to ear, he waited for the connection.

"This is a pleasant surprise, Mr. Dane," the voice of an elderly man said.

The man called himself Number One. Dane didn't know his real name, but he did know that the man, an American, was a former intelligence official who had started an organization called The Trust. His group was made up of other former intelligence officials from around the globe who pooled resources and continued the work they'd allegedly retired from, i.e. trying to keep the world from destroying itself, but, this time, without the red tape.

Number One and The Trust had proved invaluable to Dane in the past; he owed them. But first he had another favor to ask.

"Someday we'll have a conversation," Dane said, "that doesn't include bad news."

Number One chuckled. "Not in our world. How are you enjoying Montana?"

"How did you know?"

"We have eyes everywhere. You've been busy. I know why you're calling."

Now Dane smiled. He wanted to play along with the old man. "Why am I calling?"

"You've slain the demons of your past, but now Nina's are rearing their head," Number One said. "You've had an argument with her on the subject once already, and now you're wondering what to do now that a confrontation in inevitable. I offered the assistance of The Trust in both cases. Is that why you're calling?"

Dane blinked. The old man could read him like a book,

and they were thousands of miles apart from each other.

"I don't know that I'm necessarily looking for assistance," Dane said, "but something more along the lines of counseling. I collected some information on the syndicate, and I now know why Nina has been so reluctant to address this issue."

He nervously glanced back at the house to make sure she hadn't come out to see who he was talking to.

"Of course, Mr. Dane. It's a mirror of your situation, except for obvious differences, but ask yourself how would you might have felt if the official story about your father, at the time, had been the truth?"

"I'd be a little cranky too."

Number One let out a low laugh. "What is your question?"

"How do I tell her?"

"She already knows."

"How do I bring it up?"

"Delicately."

"I was hoping for something more than that."

"This is one of those cases, Mr. Dane, where you have to make it up as you go. There is no answer to your question. You're only asking me because you don't want to see her hurt, and this situation has the potential to cause a great deal of pain. Pain that she has been running from for a long time."

Dane let out a sigh. He puffed on his cigar. There wasn't anything else to talk about.

"Thanks for taking the time," he said.

"Will you require reinforcements?"

"I have my usual crew."

"Be very careful."

"We always try to not get killed."

"Indeed. I'm here for you any time, Mr. Dane. We'll be in touch again soon, I'm sure."

Dane ended the call. He didn't go into the house right away. He stayed outside, stared at the mountains, and collected his thoughts.

Dane was quiet at breakfast as Stone and McConn, on one side of the kitchen table, talked about activity in town and places to see if they had time. Nina kept glancing at Dane, silently demanding he say something. She knew he'd taken a great deal of papers from the safe of Veronica Ansemi before disposing of the woman, and she wanted to know what those papers said.

Because the nightmares hadn't stopped.

Finally, she had enough. She knew that he knew something and knew he didn't want to talk about it, but, as he'd said many times, much to her annoyance, some things had to be discussed at some point.

Might as well start now.

Nina kicked him under the table.

"Hey!"

"Why aren't you talking?" she said. She put down her coffee mug and pushed her plate away. Only bits of egg remained. She'd finished the sausage and diced potatoes, courtesy of Todd McConn, who wasn't a bad cook at all, she had to admit.

"Because I'm thinking."

"Are you thinking about how we can best recover the antiques and get paid?"

"Getting a reward for those antiques was never the reason for this, Nina, we've had this discussion already."

"What are you thinking about? What did you find at Ansemi's house?"

Dane shoved his plate away. He wasn't finished, but the look on his face suggested his appetite had flown south.

He glanced at Stone and McConn.

"You're waiting for an answer, too?"

"We didn't plan for a long-term stay," Devlin Stone said.

The legs of Dane's chair scraped the tiled floor as he pushed back. "Let's go to the living room."

Nina followed behind Dane, Stone, and McConn. It was the only way to hide what was on her face plain as day.

Chapter Thirty-Nine

"What I found at Veronica Ansemi's place," Dane said, "regards her and Mark Keller's connection to a human trafficking network, the network that needs operating funds, and expected to get those funds via the sale of stolen Iraqi antiques. The syndicate has suffered heavy losses over the last six months. The US government is cracking down on trafficking in a big way, arrests are up, smuggling routes have been smashed, and that's made it hard to sell people. Ansemi and Keller represented the US link to a syndicate that has connections in Belgrade and begins in—" Dane hesitated.

But Nina didn't.

"Moscow," she said. "It's why I'm having nightmares."

He stood before Nina, Stone, and McConn in the living room. They sat on the couch, facing him. The living room was as clean and antiseptic as the rest of the house. The furniture, at least, wasn't cheap, but the owner didn't want his guests getting too comfortable. Or he didn't want anything nice around that could be crushed during a wild party.

The papers from Ansemi's safe, and the corresponding notes Dane had made during his review, sat on a folding table to his right. He picked up a notepad and consulted his notes.

"Who is Valeri Talikov?"

He looked at Nina.

Her eyes dropped. Her shoulders seemed to sink a little.

"He's your father, isn't he?"

She nodded. "Yes, he is."

"Why the difference in your last name?" McConn said.

"It's a Russian thing," she said. "If the father's name ends in 'ov' then we add an 'a' to the daughters. It signifies that we are 'the daughter of'. It can be confusing to non-Russians but that's how it is.

She continued, "My father is the man in my nightmares. The one who tells me we'll see each other very soon. It's what I've been running from most of my adult life."

Dane tried to soften his voice so as not to sound like a military commander but wondered if he could pull it off. "We need to know the story," he said, adding: "Babe."

She raised an eyebrow at him, then turned her glance to McConn and Stone, who quietly sat, their attention on her.

She cleared her throat and sat straight.

"I had a boyfriend in college, his name was Dimitri. He was a Moscow policeman. He and I were walking along the Moscow River one night. Three men ambushed us, killed him, almost got me, but I ran fast.

"I joined the FSB," she continued, "to find the killers. The story at the time was that Dimitri was in the middle of a mafia investigation, and got too close so they killed him, but that wasn't the whole story.

"When I tracked down the three men, I shot them dead. And that's when I found out the truth.

"Dimitri wasn't just dealing with the mafia, he was dealing with human traffickers, in Moscow, who were trying to make a deal with another syndicate in Croatia—the Balkan connection. With the men I shot out of the way, the Balkans were able to slip their own people into the outfit, and the alliance was formed.

"One night, somebody left a file on my desk. I never found out who. I started reading it because I thought it was related to a new assignment. I started reading about a Moscow-based human smuggling network, and eventually reached the page that identified the major players and the ringleader. That's when I found out the leader of the syndicate was my father, Val Talikov."

She stopped talking.

Dane said, "You never knew? He wasn't exactly hiding Easter eggs."

She shook her head. "It's one of those things where you look back for signs, anything you might have missed, but no matter how much I thought back over the years, all I saw was a man who pulled the wool completely over the eyes of his family, and never once showed any indication that he wasn't the upstanding father we all thought he was."

She cleared her throat.

"It did explain why some of my colleagues at FSB always seemed to be whispering behind my back. They knew more than I did, and they thought I was there to help him, not enforce the law. My bosses thought they could use me to get to him. It was one big catastrophe waiting to happen. They really liked me when I ran away. By then I'd learned the whole story but couldn't handle it. I took off"—she paused, glanced at the faces watching her—"and found you idiots."

McConn and Stone said nothing. Dane examined his notes some more.

"Did you confront him?" Dane said.

She laughed. "He tried to get me to join the organization. Can you believe that?"

Dane delivered his next words carefully, fully aware of what they suggested.

"We can't let him continue," Dane said.

She looked at the floor again.

"I know."

"That means—"

"I know what it means."

"Can you do it?"

She looked at him sharply. "What do you think?"

"I'm not sure you can."

"You'd be wrong."

"Really?"

"Really! Ultimately he's the one responsible for Dimitri's murder; he probably manipulated me into shooting the men I killed thinking it was a sick joke; he's responsible for untold suffering, who knows how many more murders, and making my country a cesspool for criminals who are just like him, with their own daughters who are just like me! It has to stop."

"I think that's the most I've ever heard you say sober," Dane said.

"You ass!"

Dane put his notes down.

Nina's gaze smoldered and she said, "I told you I know everything. You can burn those papers the same way you burned their owner. She doesn't have half the information still jammed in my head."

Dane leaned against the table and watched her. He hoped she could manage the fury; if not, she was putting them all in danger.

Then he realized she might have thought the same thing about him during their last mission, but she'd supported him fully. He needed to return the favor.

Chapter Forty

Brussels, Belgium

Dane cleared his throat and sat down on the park bench next to an older man with a bag of breadcrumbs. He tossed the crumbs at his feet. Pigeons snarfed the crumbs off the grass. There was a whole flood of them, more pigeons than Dane had ever seen in one place, it seemed.

"You came alone," the old man said.

"Nina's having a hard time. You know, planning how best to kill her father, and all that is kind of draining."

Chirping birds mixed with the cooing pigeons. The park was very quiet, blue sky above, the sunlight tempered by strategically placed trees.

"I can imagine," the older man said.

"We're supposed to be in Moscow tonight."

"What's the plan?"

"Nina wants to see her ex-partner at FSB and make a formal statement of complaint against her father, citing everything she knows about his operations."

"Everything she knows is what they already know. They gave her the file."

"She says she learned other things after that," Dane said, "but that almost doesn't matter. Going on record, she says, will make her father reveal himself."

"She's sure?"

"That's the only thing she doesn't know, where her father is hiding. We can go around blowing away his associates and he can stay hidden somewhere and we'll never find him. If she announces herself, the corrupt thorns in FSB in general, and Moscow law enforcement in particular, will come looking for her."

"And bring her to her father?"

"One way or another, he's going to want to see his little girl once he realizes she's behind all this."

"This is the reason I wanted to see you," Number One said. He set the bag of breadcrumbs aside and pulled a folded piece of paper out of his jacket pocket.

"You and your folded paper," Dane said.

Number One ignored the remark and handed the paper to Dane, who unfolded it and read the name written there.

"The Rockabye Lounge?"

"It's a gambling club owned by Nina's father," Number One said. "It's an alternate source of income. Not huge, but it keeps the engines running when there's nothing else. Without the antiques from Iraq, he's going to go broke. If the club were somehow taken out of the equation as well, he'll lose his safety net, too."

Dane nodded and put the paper in his shirt pocket.

"It's something Nina doesn't know," Number One added.

"I'll cut her some slack since she's been out of town for a few years," Dane said. "Thanks for the tip."

"Good luck, Mr. Dane. Have a safe flight."

Moscow

Valeri Talikov steepled his fingers and let out a long sigh as he looked at the man and woman standing in front of his desk.

The city of Moscow seemed to spread out to infinity behind him, the window glass so clean only the metal frames of the building indicated there was anything between them. It was a bright day, but the mood in the office was quite glum.

"There's been no word whatsoever?" Talikov said.

He was a large man with broad shoulders and a bald head, his high cheekbones also a prominent feature. His face showed his sixty-plus years. Val Talikov had a wide variety of experience behind him prior to becoming a Moscow crime boss and leader of an international human trafficking ring.

"Thorne and Skinner have been out of touch since their last communication," the woman said, "and I think we need to admit we probably aren't going to hear from them."

"We killed Roca and his people. All of them," Val Talikov said.

"Remember," the woman replied, "they reached out to somebody. Thorne said—"

Val Talikov waved a hand. "I know what Thorne said. I'm just not sure I believe it."

The woman said nothing more. Her name was Sabina Lakatos, late of a Romanian syndicate, who'd come aboard Talikov's operation after her old boss was murdered by a rival. She'd been working with the big man for so many years, he considered her a daughter.

"Then there are our financials," the man in front of the desk said.

Val Talikov raised an eyebrow at Mikhail Kozlov. The

man had been at Talikov's side almost as long as Sabina. Kozlov often represented Talikov when the older man refused to leave his home. He was wary of being out of the safety areas he secured for himself. Outside, the enemy, whoever they were, could get to him. When he attended meetings by proxy, not so much.

"Don't say it out loud, Mikhail."

"I won't say it, sir. But eventually, somebody is going to have to."

We're done for. Those were the words Val Talikov did not want spoken. Without the antiques, without any of the infrastructure that had been blasted to smithereens by US forces in their continuing effort to crack down on human trafficking, they were done for. There was nothing else to do but pack up and find a place to hide.

"That's all," Val Talikov said. Sabina and Mikhail dutifully exited the office.

Val Talikov rotated his chair to look out the window at the bright blue sky.

He had faced many obstacles in his life, most of which he had overcome by determination and hard work. It had not been easy being the son of a legendary KGB operative, but Val had proven himself as a capable agent, with many overseas postings that yielded a ton of intelligence for the Kremlin.

After the end of the Cold War, he had used various global connections in the criminal underworld to form the nucleus of his crime syndicate, starting small with drugs and guns, finally graduating to human trafficking when the disaster of the Balkan wars opened a market of "lost people" ripe for picking. Presently he'd expanded into Asia and Africa. The "lost" were everywhere. And nobody missed them.

But now, the walls of his carefully-built house were crumbling.

And the troubling message from Joe Thorne, received weeks earlier during what should have been a simple recovery operation, meant his life might soon crumble as well.

Chapter Forty-One

The drink tray felt heavier than normal as it rested on Iona Pavlova's hand. Business at the Rockabye Lounge had fallen off ever since the "skirt change" directive from the top floor. The Rockabye Girls, of which Iona was one of several who worked the various shifts at the lounge, were known for their micro-minis that often displayed a little more than intended. But now the skirts were longer, and white blouses had replaced the tube tops, because tourists from Europe and the United States were complaining and the owners couldn't risk losing tourist money.

She chased orders from table to table, running to the bar to fill the orders, venturing back into the fray to deliver. Her section was full of stoic poker players, but not every table was full. There were plenty of empty seats; in fact, plenty of empty tables. Maybe the high rollers would come back, but as Iona handed a fellow his dry martini and noticed he had a pair of aces in his hand, she decided it might be better to start looking for another job.

She didn't mind the Rockabye, although the dim lighting sometimes made it hard to maneuver through the tables. The veterans always had to brief the new girls on how to watch where they stepped while at the same time keeping the service speedy. A haze of smoke from too many cigarettes and cigars hung just below the ceiling, and her clothes always smelled like an ash tray after work, but the filtering system kept the worst of the haze away.

She collected more orders, mostly refills, and returned to the bar. She had to wait while another server loaded up and then the bartender turned his attention to her.

While the bartender filled glasses, Iona started thinking about nursing school. Again. Maybe she should go back. Working the Rockabye was no way to make a living.

And then somebody kicked in the front door.

Klas Bogdanov ran the Rockabye Lounge for the Talikov syndicate, and he'd been in the position for five years.

Nobody liked to talk about the last guy who sat in the chair.

Bogdanov and his assistant manager, "Bones" Mikka, watched the play on a pair of big screen monitors. With the flick of a switch, Bogdanov could monitor individual tables or an entire section. They had the poker tables on both screens, casually watching the activity, both of them silent as they repeatedly counted the empty tables.

"This is ridiculous," Bogdanov finally said.

"They'll come back," Bones said. "Once they cool off, they'll come back."

"A guy can't have any fun anymore," Bogdanov said. "There ain't nothing wrong with girls in short skirts."

"The tourists said we were disrespecting women and if we didn't change, they'd find somewhere else to party."

"We were the easy target, that's why. The boss doesn't want the attention."

"That keeps attention away from us, too, you know."

Bogdanov grunted. "I suppose."

And then somebody kicked in the front door.

Nina parked the rental half a block from the Rockabye Lounge. Dane gave her a peck on the cheek, exited, and walked the rest of the way to the club.

It was a private gambling club that catered to the high rollers who wanted a more intimate setting than the big casinos provided.

His target was the building itself. He wanted to burn it down. The Talikov goons inside were a bonus.

But there were plenty of innocents inside.

Players. Workers.

He had to be careful.

The door man in front of the building recognized trouble. Dane saw his face tighten up and his hand go for the radio on his belt. Dane closed the man's mouth with a quick sucker-punch. The door man's bottom lip split, blood splattering on his white shirt. Dane slammed a fist into the man's gut, putting him on the ground. Dane snatched the SIG MCX from under his coat and kicked open the door. It swung inward, violently crashing against the wall opposite, and he marched in with the SIG leading the way.

A few faces turned his way, panic rising as somebody shouted, "He's got a gun!" and then all hell broke loose as players and servers and the bartenders screamed and ran for cover or the back door. Dane fired a burst of rounds into the ceiling, shouting, "Everybody get out!" and punctuating the line with two more bursts. He moved away from the door and across the floor to a flight of steps. The main officers waited at the time, and so did a Talikov gunman who drew on Dane with a revolver.

Dane admired the attempt. The fellow was young but looked like he knew how to handle the Smith & Wesson Model 29, the Dirty Harry gun that could blow a man's head clean off, if the myth was to be believed. But that's where Dane's attention ended. The SIG MCX spoke again, the chatter of .300 Blackout rounds stitching the gunner from crotch-to-chest, opening him like an avocado, blood and bits of flesh blasting out his back. He fell forward, sliding down the steps, leaving a trail of red with chunks in it on every step before his corpse came to a halt midway down the stairs.

Dane hustled upward, careful to avoid the gore, and kicked open the office door just as hard as he had the front.

The first man he saw, short and skinny with wire-framed glasses, aimed a .32 auto at him. Dane shot him in the shoulder. The man screamed and hit the white carpet, which was an awful choice, considering it was now stained with dude's blood.

The other fellow, larger, hunkered behind a desk and was clawing inside a drawer. He finally pulled out a pistol. Dane fired again. The man's hand disappeared in a flash of blood and bone and soon he was left grasping a stump and screaming his damn fool head off. Dane went over and kicked him unconscious.

Dane crossed to the first man, who had a hand to his wounded shoulder but hadn't tried to rise from the carpet. Dane aimed the SIG at him.

"Tell the old man we're coming for him."

The man's strained reply came out through clenched teeth.

"Who are you?"

"The party crasher."

Dane slung the MCX carbine and pulled out a road

flare. It was a crude way to start a fire, but the job would get done. He broke the tip of the first, a shower of sparks flying, following by a smoldering flame. He tossed it at the curtains on the other side of the room. The flame caught, the curtains started burning, and smoke began filling the office.

"If you can get your buddy out of here without slipping on the stairs and cracking open your skulls," Dane told the bleeding man on the floor, "more power to you."

The play area had mostly cleared out by the time Dane reached the ground floor again. He slung the MCX back under his coat and left casually, as if the Rockabye was his normal hang-out and it was time to go home.

Chapter Forty-Two

Nina powered into traffic as Dane checked their back.

"There's a lot to say for noise covering your exit," he said. Only normal traffic was behind them, the neon flash of Pulse fading in the distance. And then—

"Make a few extra turns," Dane said. There was one car, the make of which he couldn't tell in the glare of the headlamps, aggressively weaving through lanes. The car closed the distance quickly.

Nina turned onto Leningradsky Avenue and the engine grumbled as she pressed the accelerator, weaving through cars, honking, Dane gripping his seat to keep from being jostled. The headlamps of the unknown car stayed with them, now only a few cars back.

"Do we have a tail?" she said.

"For sure."

Dane faced forward, buckled up, and slapped a new mag into the SIG.

"I see them," Nina said after a quick glance in the rearview.

Dane held his breath a moment, let it out. Not a clean

getaway after all. Now the enemy was on their tail. There might be no avoiding a street fight.

He looked forward. Streetlights flashed, storefronts a blur. Nina powered through a yellow light.

"That car just turned off," she said.

Dane looked back. There were plenty of other cars.

"They're going to try and box us in."

Dane lurched as Nina made a sharp right turn. He sat forward again.

"They can't do that if they can't catch up," she said. "What's the plan if they do?"

"Shoot our way out."

"Is that the best you can do?"

"Do you have another idea?"

"The passages."

"What?"

"Tunnels under the street."

The cabin brightened as a car behind them got right on the bumper, high beams unmerciful. Dane grabbed the SIG with his finger resting on the trigger.

Another sharp turn onto Butyrskaya. The car sped onward, the street less crowded as the blocks turned to closed offices and warehouses. Dane spotted signs for the Savyolovsky railway station ahead

Nina let out a curse and slammed the brakes. Dane strained against the seatbelt. A car blasted out of an alley ahead and screeched to a stop in front of them. Nina threw the car into park and leaped out of the car, Dane behind her. Other doors opened and closed around him. Horns blared. People yelled. On his side with the greasy blacktop beneath, Dane aimed the SIG at a wheel of the car in front of them and let off a burst. The roar shook the night. The front right tire exploded, sending shrapnel and bits of rubber everywhere. Men yelled and screamed. Dane rolled to his feet and ran around the front of the car. Nina waited near the mouth of an alley.

Nina turned and started running as Dane neared. His boots pounded the pavement as he stayed behind Nina, trusting her instincts to get them out of the area.

They reached the street at the other end of the alley and kept running along the sidewalk, dodging pedestrians who expressed various levels of vitriol at being jostled by the sprinting couple. Nina cut across the street, Dane shooting a glance back as he followed. Nobody behind them.

Fenced-off construction zones along the street funneled traffic into one lane. Dane felt mildly disoriented with the blaze of bright headlamps, the nighttime darkness, and the unfamiliar territory. He stayed close to Nina, no longer looking back. His lungs burned with the exertion. The sidewalk narrowed as part of a construction closure extended onto the sidewalk. Nina powered through, knocking down one or two people, Dane leaping over one of the fallen. She turned a corner, running into a parking lot.

Nina stopped and lifted a circular manhole. She shoved the cover to one side and started down the hole, Steve following, pulling the cover back in place, his fingers almost getting crunched. He started down the ladder after Nina, who waited on a concrete walkway.

She ducked into an alcove to open another door with a key from her pocket. The door squeaked open. Dane followed her. She shut the door and bolted the lock. They stood in the dark. Dane took out his cell phone and shined a light around. A narrow tunnel indeed.

"It branches off from the sewer," she said. "We can

follow it back to the streets near the safe house."

"Nice you remembered all the tricks," he said.

She led the way once again.

Sabina Lakatos pulled a shade to cover the window behind Val Ta-likov while Mikhail Kozlov set up the laptop on the desk.

"What are you showing me?" the boss said.

"Traffic camera outside the Rockabye picked up the two who raided the place."

"One man conducted that raid."

"One man on the inside, yes," Kozlov said, "but a woman was waiting for him in a car."

Val Talikov started to sweat as Koslov typed commands and the screen filled with black-and-white footage of the street in front of the club. One car in particular stood out as a man ran from the entrance of the club to the passenger side of the car. He pulled the door shut. The driver accelerated, closing on the camera. Koslov paused the picture at the exact spot where the driver's face was highlighted by a streetlamp, and her features were clear.

Val Talikov's shoulders sank.

"Thorne was right," he said. "And now my daughter has come home."

Chapter Forty-Three

Nile Balakin checked his pockets for his keys and wallet, threw on his jacket, and clutched his battered briefcase in his left hand as he left the office and walked the short distance down the hall to the elevator.

Balakin was a senior investigator with the Moscow FSB. He'd risen from the ranks of street duty to the main office, where he oversaw a staff of five other investigators who handled the tough assignments that often needed the attention of Moscow FSB, such as counter-terrorist and counter-insurgency investigations, internal threats, and violations of federal law.

The office stayed quite busy.

The elevator descended quietly. He was probably one of the last people in the building, everybody else having gone home to their normal lives hours ago. Balakin had reports to review and file, and other mind-numbing paperwork to catch up on. It was Friday, and he and his wife had a long weekend planned where he didn't want to talk about, think about, or even remember his work.

It was a cold night and Balakin's feet hit the parking lot

asphalt hard. He hadn't been out of his shoes in over fourteen hours. The days were long and hard and all he wanted was a weekend away from telephones, urgent conferences, and one crisis after another.

He'd left his car at the far end of the parking lot near the security gate, which required a card pressed to a sensor in order to open, so Balakin frowned when he saw a woman leaning against his car and a man standing near her. The frown deepened as he examined her face in the light from a lamppost, and his throat dried up, his pulse quickening. It couldn't be, but it was. The office had been buzzing about the return of Nina Talikova ever since her face showed up on a traffic camera outside the Rockabye Lounge, but nobody believed she'd ever show up at headquarters.

"I don't believe this," Balakin said. He stopped short of the car, staring at her. "What are you doing here, Nina?"

"An old friend can't visit?"

"How did you get through the gate?"

"Really, Nile? That gate hasn't been replaced since I left, and it still has the same flaws. Anybody with three-quarters of a brain can force that gate and not set off the alarm."

Balakin took a breath to say something with his voice raised, but then stopped. He was talking to Nina Talikova. Nina the Bitch. She could rile up the calmest person in the room without breaking a sweat.

He set down his briefcase to gain a moment, then straightened again.

"Who's he?" Nile said.

"Guess."

"Steve Dane?"

"Bingo."

"Nobody was surprised you hooked up with a murderer, Nina."

"Hey!" Dane said. "I never killed anybody who didn't deserve it."

Balakin pressed his lips together. "Why are you here?"

"I am here to testify."

"About what?"

"You can't fool me, Nile. You're well aware of a certain traffic camera photo that should have made it to your desk by now." Nina laughed. "Don't look at me that way. You think that was an accident?"

"You're here for your father."

"I'm here to do what I should have done a long time ago."

"What, exactly?"

"Provide evidence of his crimes so the FSB can either organize a proper investigation or go straight for an arrest and interrogation."

Balakin laughed. "Nina, we're in Moscow. Your father is protected."

"My father is on the ropes, thanks to the Americans. The whole organization is in shambles because they don't have any money. We cut off their last source. Now it's time to finish him off."

"He won't spend a day in jail, regardless."

"Who said anything about jail?"

"You're serious?"

"Nile, it's me you're talking to."

"Right. And I remember when you ran away rather than stay and fight, and I remember when you hurt a lot of people because they felt personally betrayed."

"They never trusted me anyway."

"I did. You hurt me, Nina. We were partners. We'd already gone through a lot together, but you couldn't take five minutes to talk to me about what you were going through?"

Balakin wasn't sure what surprised him more, the fact that Nina Talikova was in front of him, or that she'd been stunned silent by his statement.

She blinked a few times. Finally: "I'm sorry, Nile."

Balakin shrugged. "You're Russian. I wasn't terribly surprised."

"That can't always be the excuse," Nina said.

"You've grown."

"A lot," she said. "And now it's time to be a big girl and tell you about my father's crimes."

"We have everything."

"Not everything. We've picked up some more along the way, international stuff, direct threats to the Motherland and the West stuff. There's more to this than a former KGB fat cat being protected by his old masters."

"A statement from you won't yield much. It will be purged, sealed, lost, something, so your father can get away. He'll close the syndicate and go into hiding somewhere until he can rebuild."

"You're not paying attention, Nile," Nina said. "I don't expect the FSB to do anything other than take credit and clean up the bodies."

"What?"

"You know, acting on a tip from a confidential informant, you and an FSB strike team raid a certain place, to be determined, engage suspects in a shootout when they resist your orders, and, oops, one of the bodies happens to be the kingpin of an international people smuggling operation."

Balakin laughed. "When forensics traces all the bullets, they'll find none of them will have been fired by FSB-approved weapons."

"We're Russians," Nina said. "We tell people what

the facts are."

Balakin sighed. "I'm meeting my wife for a long weekend. Not tonight."

"We don't have a lot of time, Nile."

"No."

"Call your wife and tell her you'll be an hour or two late. Won't be longer than that. It's Friday night. You'll be there before midnight and still have the weekend and it will be a better weekend because you'll know there's a prize about to be handed to you on a platter."

Balakin sighed again, glancing at Steve Dane, who remained stoic as Nina talked. "Will he be joining us?"

"He stays with me," Nina said. "Always."

Balakin picked up his briefcase. "All right. We basically have the building to ourselves, so you picked a good time."

"Wasn't an accident, Nile."

"Of course not. Follow me."

Balakin turned and started walking back to the headquarters building. He did not look back to see if Nina and Dane were following.

Chapter Forty-Four

"I figured you'd want some tea," Balakin said.

Dane took the offered mug. "Much appreciated, but you didn't have to go through the trouble."

"You're just a decoration?"

"Tonight, yes."

"Well you might as well be comfortable. Have a seat and I'll be back with the recording gear."

Balakin walked away.

Nina already sat in the interview room at the single table in the center, hands on her lap. Dane eased into a corner chair that had a hard seat and immediately made his rear end sore. The cold steel walls were bare, the room designed for intimidation, telling suspects that they were about to be tossed into an abyss from which there was no escape, so they better come clean and try and make it a little easier on themselves.

He watched Nina stare at her hands and move her thumbs back and forth. He knew better than to ask what she was thinking, but he had a pretty good idea.

They'd both taken the same path when confronted with

a dragon they couldn't immediately slay and required time and space for their subconscious minds to prepare them for a return engagement. She'd supported him when it was his time; now he was going to support her.

Presently Balakin returned with a microphone, digital recorder, and a notepad.

He placed the microphone in front of Nina, plugged the cord into the recorder, and pressed a button.

He asked Nina to tell her story.

She didn't stop speaking for over an hour. She presented papers obtained from the Ansemi safe in San Isabel, and information she'd collected over the years, recited from memory. Balakin took notes and let the recorder run. His face showed a certain weariness as she spoke that Dane more than understood. He'd get the credit for the kill, but, right now, he was being used by somebody unashamedly planning to break the law he was sworn to enforce.

Dane didn't envy Balakin at all.

The biting chill off the water made Dane wish for a heavier jacket.

Stone had managed to secure a safe house near Severnoye Tushimo Park, the one-story home with the wrap-around porch near the shore of the Moscow Canal. The water wasn't far, but without direct light, the water looked black, resembling a dark chasm from which one could fall through into infinity. On the opposite shore, cargo ships lined industrial docks, tall unloading cranes silent, but lighted against the night sky, their tops reaching for the stars.

Dane, via his La Galera cigar, sent smoke signals into the sky himself.

The forest surrounding the house provided excellent cover and concealment, which had been the utmost priority for Stone when locating the safe house. They expected to be attacked at any moment, Balakin having submitted Nina's report along official channels before, finally, getting a chance to leave for real, and get on with his weekend.

The sliding glass door opened behind him. Music from inside filtered out, then went silent as the door slid shut. Dane did not turn around. He knew Nina's light footsteps when he heard them.

She joined him at the wooden rail and looked out over the water.

"It looks kind of gross during the day," she said, her voice low. There was no reason to speak loudly considering their isolation. "The port on the other side is gray and ugly, and it makes the water look ugly too."

"You just don't like it here," Dane said.

"I'm trying very hard to replace bad memories and experiences with good ones. There were many good times, before the bad times."

Dane nodded.

"I borrowed Stone's Derringer," she said.

"I didn't know he had one."

"He's been keeping it behind his back, clipped to his belt, since we rescued him from Colombia. I strapped it inside my underwear. I have a feeling I'll need it."

Dane laughed. "Odd place for it."

"Not really. I know my father. If he orders me searched, he won't let his goons touch my lady part."

Dane considered the strategy and puffed on his cigar. "Makes sense, actually. You think your father will be nice?"

"He needs to know what we did with the antiques from Iraq. He won't hurt me. You, on the other hand, are probably going to be tortured half to death."

"Aren't I always? We can't end the story without a good

torture scene, and I always seem to get picked for that."

She raised an eyebrow.

"Most of the time," Dane added.

"That's so your brilliant friends and your beautiful lover, who manage to avoid capture, can rescue you."

They laughed. Dane put an arm around her, and she leaned her head on his shoulder.

"It's going to be all right," he said.

"I know. But it also won't ever be the same."

"It hasn't been the same for a long time."

"There was always the thought in the back of my mind that it wasn't true," she said. "That there was an explanation, some sort of secret plan behind the masquerade."

"I know."

"And I'm amazed I haven't been hitting the bottle since we got here."

"You're taking after me, after last time."

"I suppose. I'll make up for it when we're done, though, I'm sure."

"You could try not doing that."

"I could," she agreed. Then: "What's that noise?"

Dane listened. Faint, but growing louder. "Engines."

"Car and boat."

"Tell Stone and McConn to get ready, they're coming."

She pulled away from Dane and raced inside the house. The music stopped.

Dane clamped his cigar in the right side of his mouth, took out his .45, and snapped back the action.

"Come and get it, boys," he said.

A boat cleared the shoreline trees off to his left. And then the spotlight hit him. Furious words in Russian echoed over a loudspeaker. Dane tightened his grip as more commotion from the front of the house reached his ears.

The enemy had arrived.

With half a platoon.

Dane laughed. This time, the odds were so far out of his favor, he might as well not have bothered to show up. He ignored the commands from the loudspeaker, raised the Detonics and fired twice. A return burst splintered the porch rail as he ducked, spit out his cigar, and ran back inside the house, only to stop short as he faced a line of armed men in black who already had Nina, Stone, and McConn on their knees.

The leader of the group said, "This doesn't end well if you don't cooperate, Mr. Dane."

Dane dropped his gun on the floor. More gunmen from the boat charged onto the back porch, heavy boots thudding onto the wooden planks, and into the house. The room suddenly felt very crowded, and very small.

Dane glanced at the men behind him, then turned to the men in front of him. "Take us to your leader," he said, "and we'll get this wrapped up."

One of the gunmen came over and bashed Dane in the face with the stock of his rifle.

Everything turned black as Dane landed hard on the carpet.

Chapter Forty-Five

Nina shifted in the back seat of the black BMW sedan, cleared her throat, and said to the man next to her, "Was it necessary to hit Steve?"

Val Talikov let out a low laugh. "Establishing authority, my dear."

One of the gunmen shut Nina's door, and the car started off. Two other cars trailed behind, one of which contained Steve. Her father had left three troopers at the house with a tied-up Stone and McConn; the boat crew had fully departed. Her father traveled with quite the security force, and for a good reason, she figured, considered she and Steve had made it look like an army was after them.

They sat beside each other in stony silence as the car's engine grumbled. She found herself incredibly calm, the opposite of what she'd expected. She had to shift again. The Derringer pistol stuck in her panties was digging into her abdomen. She was calm enough to wonder if that had been such a good idea.

"You look well," her father said.

"And you."

"I may have put on a couple of pounds since you saw me last."

"If you suggest I have," Nina said, "you'll be dead before we get to wherever we're going."

Val Talikov laughed, and not a short laugh, a good heavy laugh just short of a guffaw.

"You have not changed a bit."

Nina did not smile.

"Where are we going?" she said.

"A place where we can talk privately."

"What are you going to do with Steve?"

"He won't be damaged," her father said, "as long as you cooperate."

"I think you've misjudged the both of us."

"How so?"

"We always have a plan."

"And what is your plan this time, as you face overwhelming odds, and your own flesh and blood?"

"Not telling," she said, "but I promise that neither of us plans to be buried in Moscow."

Nina folded her arms.

They rode on in silence.

Sabina Lakatos and Mikhail Kozlov, Val Talikov's assistants, dragged Dane by his arms across a dusty floor and dropped him. He groaned, staying flat while his vision spun and the lump behind his head throbbed. He finally pushed himself onto his side and sat up, shoulders slumped, hands limp in his lap.

He looked up at Mikhail Koslov. The tall Russian still held the rifle he'd smashed Dane's head with, and Dane saw a hint of blood on the buttstock.

"You didn't have to hit me," Dane said.

"Sure I did," the Russian said.

Dane glanced at the woman, her hair down over her shoulders, form-fitting black top, black leather pants and black boots making up her outfit.

"Did you escape from a motorcycle club or something?"

"Stop talking."

"Why?"

Sabina's left leg lashed out, striking Dane on the side of the head. He toppled over, unmoving. More pain. He liked pain. It meant he wasn't dead. He let out the appropriate noises and raised himself on his right arm.

"You kick like a girl," Dane said.

She moved forward again, but Koslov grabbed her arm, holding her back.

"You're supposed to tie me to a chair." He looked around. Bare floor, no walls, cement posts holding up the ceiling. Dirty windows further away. They were in a building, an abandoned building, and nothing beyond the windows indicated where. Dane had to admit that he wouldn't know where they were anyway, even if he could see a street sign. He wasn't familiar with Moscow at all.

He looked at the woman again. She carried no rifle, but a Makarov pistol rode on her right hip.

"One of you going to get the chair? Or dangle me over the edge of the roof? Come on, this is the torture scene. You're supposed to get creative."

The woman smiled and reached behind her back. She showed Dane a small dagger, with a shiny blade. Pulling strands of her lovely blonde hair forward, she wiped with the dagger, and tossed the hair in front of Dane.

"Oh, we'll get creative," she said. "Don't you worry about that."

A chill ran through Dane's body. He wasn't going to get out of this one as easily as in the past.

The room was dark, with a single light bulb hanging from the ceiling, the light focused in the center of the room and leaving the area beyond in shadow. Nina's father leaned against a poker table on rickety legs. She stood in the light.

His face was half in shadow.

Just like in her nightmares.

"Now, Nina, we need to have a talk."

Nina stood with folded arms, her weight on her right leg, trying to look aloof.

She'd watched the other two drag Steve away; where she didn't know. The only thing that consoled her at this moment was that she couldn't hear him screaming. Were they beating him, or trying to get him to reveal the location of the Iraqi antiques?

"What do you want to talk about?"

Val Talikov smiled. "You're still a tough girl. That makes me proud. Running around with that American fool hasn't softened you one bit."

Nina said nothing. She was screaming inside her head but did not want to reveal that to the old man.

"I want to know where the antiques are," he said.

A scream. Short, sharp, piercing.

Nina didn't flinch. She needed to buy time. Time to draw the Derringer and plant a slug between her father's eyes. But the weapon only held two rounds of .22 Magnum ammunition, and there were more armed men outside, she'd counted at least six, and the two assistants, one of whom had an automatic rifle. The woman only carried a pistol. If Nina needed both .22 shells for her father, how would she handle the remaining threats?

Sweat trickled down her neck.

"A lot of people have died because of those antiques,"

she said.

"I know."

"They don't belong to you."

Val Talikov laughed. "There's a substantial reward for their return, isn't there? Is that what you have in mind?"

"It's better than selling them to fund your disgusting business."

"Nobody misses the people I sell, Nina. They're nobody."

"They mean something to somebody. They're human beings."

Val Talikov might have shrugged. She couldn't tell since there was so much of his body she couldn't see.

"They're people who are lost, in mind, body and spirit."

"And that gives you the right to make them slaves of one form or another?"

"Maybe your American friend has changed you, Nina."

Another scream, this one longer, ending on a note of total agony.

Nina took a deep breath.

"One thing's for sure," Nina said. "I have no idea who you are anymore. How did you hide this side of you for so long?"

"It was easy," Val Talikova said. "Your mother did most of the work, keeping you in the dark."

"Did she know?"

"She knew I wasn't an honest businessman, but she didn't know what kind of businessman I was."

"You're admitting you're a criminal."

"I am a criminal. I've never felt any shame in that. We have to make our way in the world somehow, Nina, my dear."

"That's a terrible excuse. There are plenty of ways to survive."

"What was a former KGB man to do? I couldn't take us to America. By the end of the Cold War, there was no reason to defect. They wouldn't have wanted me. I wasn't powerful enough. I made other choices instead. Choices that you benefitted from, from food and shelter to your education."

"Are you suggesting I owe you something?"

"I'm suggesting you don't know the whole story, the reason I do these things."

"Mom has been gone a long time. I've been an adult for a long time. You kept running your business for your own selfish reasons. Don't try and make this my fault."

Val Talikov sighed.

"And here we are," Nina said.

"Here we are indeed. Where are my antiques?"

Chapter Forty-Six

"I'm not telling."

Another scream.

"If you don't tell me, Mr. Dane won't walk out of here alive."

"What about me? What will you do? Sell me to somebody in the Middle East?"

Her father shook his head.

"Why don't you ground me and take away my phone privileges?"

Val Talikov laughed.

"You hold up well, my dear, but every time Mr. Dane screams, I can see in your eyes that it hurts you, too. Make no mistakes. I am your father, and I know you better than you know yourself, despite the length of time we haven't seen each other."

"You can hurt Steve all you want," she said. "Remember I told you about our plan. We have friends everywhere, friends in high places. And in low places."

"Where are they now? Where are these friends you boast about?"

Nina swallowed.

"Are you waiting for them to crash through the front door, and rescue you at the last possible moment? How are they going to get past the men I stationed outside?"

"We might surprise you."

"You might. But I don't think so. Not this time."

Nina tried to respond, but her mouth wouldn't move.

Steve screamed again.

Sabina held the knife at the ready while Koslov slung his weapon and went to a wall with a portion of the sheet rock cut away to expose cables. He pulled a line of cable out of the wall, called the woman over to make a few cuts, and used the table to bind Dane's wrists and ankles. He lay on the dusty floor, hurting all over, and unable to resist. At the last minute, Sabina stripped off Dane's belt. So much for his hidden razor blade. She tossed the belt aside. She stood over Dane long enough to straddle his midsection. She sliced open the front of his shirt, flinging the buttons this way and that, exposing his chest and stomach.

"How nice," she said, running a hand up his belly to his chest. Dane squirmed. Her hand was cold, her skin dry. "Your lady friend must really like you."

The knife moved in her other hand, one quick swipe, the blade cutting fiercely into his stomach, drawing blood. Dane yelled. The hot blood trickled down his side and pooled underneath.

"Death by a thousand cuts, Mr. Dane," she said, leaning down to look in his eyes. Her hot breath touched his neck. "Is that creative enough for you?"

The knife moved again.

Dane screamed.

And again.

Dane screamed.

And again.

He shifted back and forth beneath the woman. She couldn't see his hands moving against the cable holding his wrists together. The wire insulation didn't quite dig into his skin, and the knot wasn't very tight. Cable makes lousy rope.

He wasn't aware when Mikhail Koslov left the room.

"Beat Steve all you want," Nina said, feeling like she was repeating herself uselessly, and talking desperately. Anything to figure a way out! "Your infrastructure is destroyed. We finished what the Americans started. You'll be indicted, even in death. With or without the antiques, your organization is finished."

"You're spinning wheels, Nina. Stop wasting my time."

Movement behind her. Nina turned. The man with the rifle. She didn't know his name. He casually approached, regarding her with disinterest, as he took his place beside her father. He carried his rifle leisurely.

Nina faced her father, hooking her thumbs in either pocket.

"We're done," she said. "It's time to do your worst." She paused, adding: "Papa."

Val Talikov's face hardened. "This is a shame. When you left me, Nina, I found other children who are devoted to me, such as Mikhail here, and Sabina, who is dealing with Dane." He raised his right hand and snapped his fingers. "Do it, Mikhail."

Koslov flicked off the rifle's safety and started to raise the weapon to his shoulder.

"Papa," Nina said, "you never checked me for a gun."

Nina's left hand pulled at the waistband of her jeans,

while her right hand went between her legs, pulling out the .22 Derringer with such speed that her father took a step into the light, incredulity spreading across his face as she fired. The .22 Magnum barked once. A neat red hole appeared in the center of Val Talikov's head, a comma of blood forming quickly, turning into a trickle that formed a red line between his eyes, curving as it reached his nose, and by then the old man fell forward like a chopped tree. The floor shook when his heavy body landed face first.

Nina shifted her aim and fired the second round. Mikhail Koslov's left eye popped. He screamed, Nina diving to the floor as the automatic weapon fired, flame flashing briefly from the barrel before he, too, joined his boss on the floor.

Nina let go of the Derringer and ran to Koslov, rolling his body over, snatching up the rifle. How many rounds gone? She patted him for a spare magazine and found one in a back pocket. Replacing the partially spent mag, she started forward. Time to find Steve.

And get them both out of here.

Automatic gunfire echoed.

Sabina Lakatos stopped, the knife midway between her and Dane's chest, raising her head at the sound.

"Game over," Dane said.

She snapped her eyes back to him. Dane hands swung up from behind his back. He slammed his palms against the woman's ears. She screamed, recoiling, Dane rolling fast, pinning her beneath his weight. She slashed once with the knife. Dane blocked her wrist, twisting, the knife falling, his free right fist slamming into her face once, twice. Her upper lip split. Another punch. Her cheek split, lines of blood ruining the otherwise pretty landscape. Both hands found her neck, cutting off her next yell as he squeezed and slammed her head against the floor.

Her arms and legs flailed ineffectively. And within moments, she stopped moving, her dead eyes staring at Dane in defiance.

Dane stood up, gasping.

"Am I awful," Nina said, "for saying how hot you look with your shirt open?"

She stood in the doorway holding the automatic rifle.

"It's okay," Dane said, grabbing the Makarov pistol from Sabina's hip. "I always look hot."

Chapter Forty-Seven

They hustled down the stairwell. The elevators apparently didn't work, as they hadn't been used to get them to the upper floors. The troops outside stood between them and freedom. They needed to get past the gunners, and into one of the cars.

Dane hoped Stone and McConn were still in one piece.

One more obstacle before they were done.

Dane led the way with the Makarov pistol clutched in both hands, his shirt, in tatters, hanging on his torso. He ignored the pain. He felt less of it now that he was free, and adrenaline coursed through his veins, supercharging his reactions.

They reached the ground floor and peeked through the doorway to the building lobby, empty like the rest of the structure, the floor dusty, debris here and there. No real cover or concealment, though. That was the bad news.

And Dane had to admit he wasn't finding any good news at all.

"Here they come," Dane said.

Having heard the shooting, and no word from the boss,

the troopers were now investigating. Six of them total, all carrying automatic rifles like Nina carried.

Dane ducked back, holding the pistol close to his body. Nina stepped further back, ready with the rifle.

When the stairwell door opened, Dane fired twice. The gunfire was deafening in the confined space, bouncing off the walls. The first man in the doorway took both rounds high in the chest, falling back; Dane fired twice more. Second man, behind the first, dropped hard. The rest of the team started shouting. Dane ignored them. He grabbed the ankles of the first man and dragged him through the doorway, trading the pistol for the rifle.

"Now!" he shouted.

Dane and Nina stormed through the door and into the lobby, the muzzles of their rifles seeking targets. The remaining four shooters had spread out, grouped by two. Dane sighted on his pair and the rifle bucked against his shoulder, two steady bursts. One down. He shifted aim and stitched the second gunman stomach to chest.

Pivoting, he and Nina fired at the same time, cutting down the last two before their weapons ran dry.

They dropped the rifles and quickly collected two more, along with spare ammunition.

Then they ran.

Outside, into the cold night. The black sedans lay ahead, silent, waiting. The first vehicle they checked had the keys in the ignition.

Nina drove.

Devlin Stone and Todd McConn had no doubt they wouldn't see sunrise once the boss called.

The trio of troopers made no acknowledgement of them whatsoever as they stood guard, the television on, everybody waiting for the phone call that would tell them that the boss had what he wanted, and the two hostages could be disposed of.

Stone hoped Nina had made good use of his Derringer, because he sure wished he had it now.

The call never came.

When they heard a car engine out front, the TV was turned off, the troops gathered their weapons, and debated which one of them would go outside and check who the new arrival was.

Then the door crashed open.

San Francisco, California

Detective Gino Vicini took his coffee and paper to a corner table and sat down. He was halfway through the sports section when another man joined him. He set down the paper and smiled.

"Dane," the inspector said, "what brings you back here?"

Dane opened the tote bag he carried and handed Vicini a box of La Galera cigars. "As promised."

"Thanks. You look a little rough."

"You should see the other gal. How's your partner?"

"Okay. He's getting help for a gambling problem. I got to him before anybody official found out. Hopefully he'll stay away from the card tables now."

"Uh-huh." Dane pulled a bottle of Gentleman Jack from the tote. "Make sure he gets this."

"Forgive and forget?"

"Sure. And you can consider the Wexler case closed."

"I don't want to know," Vicini said.

"Yes, you do."

"Yes, I do," Vicini said, "but don't tell me."

Dane only smiled, knowing Vicini would never understand what happened in Moscow, or why, or its effect on Dane and Nina.

"You staying long?" the cop said.

"No."

"Good. I hear you're wanted in Arizona for jumping bail, so we never spoke." They shook hands. "Thanks for the stogies."

"Anytime," Dane said.

"And if you ever need anything—"

"I will. So long, Inspector."

Dane joined Nina outside the Starbucks and they started walking, turning right on Howard Street with The Embarcadero's ocean view ahead.

"I've been thinking of all that loot buried underground," she said.

"Same here. I thought we'd call Len Lukavina at CIA and let him know about it, and then get the recovery process started. We'll make sure it goes back where it belongs."

"How long before we get the reward money?"

"Is that all you can think about right now?"

She smiled weakly but made no other comment.

She hadn't said much since they left Russia, Stone and McConn going their separate ways, leaving the two of them to settle accounts in San Francisco.

Dane knew better than to push her to talk about what happened. She'd open up when she was ready. If ever. It was enough to know that, maybe, her demons were finally vanquished same as his, and they could carry on with their lives however they saw fit.

For Dane, there was only one thing to do. Keep on fighting. There were plenty of underdogs that needed a champion, and he wanted to be that champion, because he could.

They stopped at the end of the sidewalk, the Embarcadero directly in front of them, once again full of cars and trollies. The Bay Bridge towered over them, Treasure Island in the center of the bay. Joggers ran along the sidewalk. Dane and Nina stopped at a railing and watched the water. Seagulls buzzed overhead.

"Do you want to stay in San Francisco for a while?" Nina said.

"Do you?"

"Not really. This place smells funny."

"I couldn't agree more," Dane said.

Nina gestured to their right. "There's a bar over there. Let's get a drink."

Before he could argue, she was halfway there.

A Look At: Terminal Memory: A Sam Raven Thriller

SAM RAVEN BATTLES THE ENEMIES JACK REACHER'S AFRAID OF. . .

Three years after a daring escape from a jihadists' camp, ex-CIA officer Mara Cole is a target once more. She's alone, on the run, and in need of a friend.

Sam Raven is tracking Mara's hunters for a different reason – he's on a mission of vengeance. A man with dark secrets, bound to Mara by shared history, they join forces to fight back. Together, they play a deadly game of chess through the back alleys of London, to the bright lights of Marseille, and the desert hell of Afghanistan opium fields, risking everything as they move closer to the truth.

With each feign and attack, they find the answers they seek lie deep in Mara's memories of captivity, torture, and betrayal – secrets to a conspiracy at the heart of the US Intelligence community, and men who will do anything to protect their power.

From the author of the Scott Stiletto series comes an exciting new hero! Sam Raven is grittier, deadlier, and you better not stand in his way.

"Tom Cruise, forget Mission Impossible. Sam Raven is your new franchise." – Rebecca Forster, author of the Finn O'Brien Thrillers

AVAILABLE NOW

About the Author

A twenty-five year veteran of radio and television broadcasting, Brian Drake has spent his career in San Francisco where he's filled writing, producing, and reporting duties with stations such as KPIX-TV, KCBS, KQED, among many others. Currently carrying out sports and traffic reporting duties for Bloomberg 960, Brian Drake spends time between reports and carefully guarded morning and evening hours cranking out action/adventure tales. He lives in California with his wife and two cats, and when he's not writing he is usually blasting along the back roads in his Corvette with his wife telling him not to drive so fast, but the engine is so loud he usually can't hear her.